"What do you know about a textile mill?"

Jared's question was sharp.

"Nothing," Holly said. "But I can learn."

"That's rubbish." He looked uneasy and annoyed. "All right, so we're partners. That's been wished on us. And I accept your half interest. But I'm in charge of things and I warn you I don't intend to—"

"To have an ignorant woman interfering?" Holly put in.

"Quite," he said crisply.

"Don't worry, Jared. I won't make a nuisance of myself. But I can't accept a share of the profits without doing something to earn it. Partners, you said so yourself."

"I'm not worried," he barked. "And I'm sure you're not going to make a nuisance of yourself—I'll see to that!"

Books by Marjorie Lewty

HARLEQUIN ROMANCE

HARLEQUIN PRESENTS

These books may be available at your local bookseller.

Don't miss any of our special offers. Write to us at the following address for information on our newest releases.

Harlequin Reader Service
P.O. Box 52040, Phoenix, AZ 85072-2040
Canadian address: P.O. Box 2800, Postal Station A,
5170 Yonge St., Willowdale, Ont. M2N 6J3

Lovers' Knot

Marjorie Lewty

Harlequin Books

TORONTO • NEW YORK • LONDON
AMSTERDAM • PARIS • SYDNEY • HAMBURG
STOCKHOLM • ATHENS • TOKYO • MILAN

Original hardcover edition published in 1984
by Mills & Boon Limited

ISBN 0-373-02678-1

Harlequin Romance first edition March 1985

CHAPTER ONE

FROM the crush of bodies milling around Arrivals at Heathrow Terminal Three she picked him out immediately. He was the one standing absolutely still. Only his eyes moved with lazy arrogance over the stream of hot, jaded passengers as they passed him, lugging hand-baggage, manipulating trolleys. He was very tall, well over six feet, with the broad shoulders and muscular thighs of an athlete. He wore a putty-coloured safari jacket and close-fitting trousers. His hair was very dark, thick and wiry and brushed carelessly away from a wide, bony forehead, and the way he stood there, watchful, his head inches above the heads of everyone around, he might have owned the whole place and be checking on the way it was functioning.

A formidable man, Holly thought. Tough. And although that was what she had been expecting, her heart sank a little. 'Hard as nails,' Paul had described his stepbrother to her. 'A right bastard, is our Jared.'

She couldn't expect him to pick her out as quickly and certainly from among the crowd as she had picked him, and she felt a slight shock, therefore, when his eyes lit on her and immediately he sauntered across towards her.

She parked her trolley and waited, standing slim and straight and composed, and although she didn't know it, she had a grace and a youthful dignity that made her stand out from the passing crowd just as surely as did the man coming towards her. As he reached her she saw that his eyes were grey, the colour of gunmetal, and they were looking her over with an expression that made her inside squeeze up with something that felt like fear, but most certainly wasn't. There was no reason for her to fear Jared Kent.

He has almost reached her now and his steely grey eyes were moving over her from head to foot. Yes, Paul's brother was a bastard all right; you could tell them a mile off, Holly thought. She recognised that expression in a man's eyes—a sort of patronising contempt for her sex as a whole—while willing, of course, to make use of its members in any way that suited them.

She was a tall girl, but he towered over her. 'You're Holly?' It was a statement rather than a question.

She caught her breath. She hadn't expected a voice like that from him—low and deep and definitely sexy. To be in character he should have sounded harsh and disdainful. That was how he had sounded on the phone when she spoke to him on Tuesday from Mexico City. But you could never tell on the telephone, could you?

On the plane she had rehearsed what she would say to him, how she would be very quiet, very dignified. She knew it was going to be unnerving, meeting Paul's stepbrother for the first time. She would need every bit of the confidence she had acquired in her twenty-three years of standing on her own feet. The last few months had shaken that confidence severely, and now was the time to regain it. But meeting those piercing grey eyes she found her mouth drying up. 'H-how did you recognise me?' she stammered.

He gestured disdainfully towards the black suit that

made Holly's slight figure look even more ethereal, and the little black pillbox hat with the fuzz of veiling that crowned the smooth mink-brown sweep of her hair.

'Widow's weeds,' he said laconically. 'Isn't that what they used to be called? I thought they'd gone out with Queen Victoria.'

She gasped. What a beastly thing to say to her, and what a beastly man who could say such a thing! She knew from Paul that he had never been close to his stepbrother, but that snide remark was unforgivable. As a matter of fact she hadn't bought the little black suit specially, it was her business suit. She had splashed out on it in the spring, when she knew she was going to Mexico as David Behrens's P.A. After the way she had parted from David she had never wanted to see the thing again, but she had worn it today in deference to Paul's mother when they met, and because, in spite of everything that had happened, she was mourning for Paul in an odd sort of way. Mourning for the waste of his youth; mourning for the wonderful golden boy he should have been—that she had believed he was when she married him three months ago. Mourning, perhaps, for her own ghastly mistake in marrying him.

Jared Kent took the handle of the trolley, containing her two heavy cases and hand baggage. 'My car's parked a good distance away.' He glanced at Holly's pale face, the delicate skin of her cheeks scarcely touched with colour, the dark smudges under her soft brown eyes evidence of the stress of the last two weeks. 'Can you walk?'

Resentment spiked through her fatigue. What would you do if I said no? she thought. Pick me up and dump me on the trolley too? He looked capable of it and the thought of feeling those muscular arms close round her made her wince and draw away from him, saying shortly, 'Of course I can walk. I'm not an invalid!'

He stood looking her over, frowning. 'No, I didn't suppose you were.' He paused, then added slowly, 'I suppose I ought to offer my condolences—very remiss of me not to have done it before.'

'Thank you,' said Holly stiffly. It was the first time he had referred directly to Paul's death. When Paul's mother had written to her, a scrawled, heartbroken, almost unintelligible screed after the accident, this man hadn't even bothered to put in a note. Of course he didn't know her, but then his stepmother didn't know her either, yet she could write with acceptance of her as one of the family. But Jared Kent meant to consider her an interloper, that was for sure.

'Let's go, then,' he said. He strode through the Heathrow terminal, a tall, dynamic, intimidating figure, trundling the heavy trolley as if it were a featherweight. Holly followed behind as he scythed his way through the crowd, up in a lift, along a passage, then another lift, apparently expecting everyone to fall back and make way for him. Arrogant beast, Holly thought, and he might have asked me if I'd like a drink or something to eat before we got to his car. If they were driving up to his home in the Lakes tonight they would be a considerable time on the way.

They reached the car at last, on the second floor of the car-park. It looked like the man himself—large and black and intimidating. Jared stowed her luggage in the boot and opened the passenger door for her, and she climbed in and sank into the recesses of a deep leather seat, keeping her eyes straight in front of her on the dashboard, groping for the seat-belt and clicking it hastily into its slot in case he felt it necessary to do it for her. The prospect of his hands touching her filled her with something that was almost panic.

'All right?' He glanced at her briefly and without waiting for an answer turned the key of the self-starter. The powerful engine roared into life, sending shock-waves of booming sound through the enclosed car-park. Holly sat back and tried to relax. This was going to be a long and very unpleasant journey, but if she kept her cool and didn't react to his calculated indifference she could get through it. There was no point in fighting with him. All she intended to do was to meet Paul's mother, and perhaps comfort her if she could, and then get away from the family as quickly as possible and start making a new life for herself. She closed her eyes as the car roared and growled its way through the late-evening London traffic. The long flight from Mexico City was having its disorientating effect and she longed for sleep.

After a time she was aware that the engine-note had settled down to a steady purr and she opened her eyes to find that they were speeding along the motorway. She glanced at the digital clock on the dash, which read 20:32. Half past eight, and the September sky was already nearly dark.

She turned her head cautiously to look at the man beside her, his profile outlined against oncoming headlights—the dominant nose, the jutting chin. Everyone's idea of a captain of industry! If she could ridicule him in her own mind it might be easier to cope with his indifference. No, it was more than indifference, it was not much short of active hostility. She wondered why he should feel like that about a girl he didn't know, who had happened to marry his stepbrother, even if he had disliked that stepbrother. It seemed an exaggerated and senseless attitude.

Not that it mattered to her; their lives would meet only very briefly. Surely he didn't imagine she was going to park herself on him and his stepmother for any length of time? She shuddered at the very idea.

'You've been asleep,' he said, not turning his head, and the sound of that deep, sexy voice, so utterly out of keeping with the rest of the man, made her fingers curl up into her palms. 'We'll stop off at the next pull-in place for a coffee. We've some way to go yet.'

He wasn't suggesting, he was telling her. Holly didn't demur; she was feeling more exhausted and miserable every second and a coffee might help her to get through the rest of the drive. Soon the lights of a motorway service station twinkled out of the dusk, and Jared drew in and backed the big car with a nonchalant twist of his wrist into a tight space between two Minis.

The self-service café was hot and crowded. Jared led the way between the aisles to the only table that was empty, pushing aside an overflowing ashtray with distaste.

Holly slid into a seat. Her legs didn't feel too reliable; it must be all those hours sitting in the plane. Jared stood looming above her. 'Black or white?' he asked. 'Anything to eat?'

The thought of food was nauseating. 'Just black coffee, please.'

She watched him stride away to the counter, pausing to throw a couple of words towards a sulky-looking girl in a pink overall, who came over immediately and removed the ashtray from the table.

Jared returned and set a beaker of coffee before her. He sat down opposite and removed his own coffee from the tray, together with a loaded plate—two thick packets of sandwiches and a large jam doughnut. 'Didn't manage to fit in lunch,' he found it necessary to explain, unwrapping the first of the packets.

For some reason the fact that he had chosen a jam doughnut for himself made him seem almost like a human being. 'It was good of you to come all this way to meet me,' Holly said.

He shrugged. 'I had to come to London on business—it was easy enough to fit it in.' He applied his attention to his sandwiches.

Holly shook inside with impotent fury. Of course—she mustn't be allowed to imagine that he would put himself out on her behalf, must she? She gulped the hot, black coffee and determined not to try to be polite to him again.

He finished off the sandwiches and the doughnut at an incredible speed and sat back, regarding her with an assessing look in his gunmetal grey eyes that made her inside clench.

'So—you're the girl who finally got Paul to the altar,' he mused. 'Or I expect it was a registrar's table. I must say you're very presentable.' The grey eyes passed insolently over her. 'I wonder why he didn't consider it necessary to let us know at the time that he'd got married.'

That took Holly by surprise. 'But he did—he wrote to his mother.'

Jared shook his head. 'He didn't, you know. Paul's never been much of a letter writer. The first she heard of it was when Luis Ferida telephoned to tell her of Paul's fatal accident. Apparently he mentioned you—as Paul's wife—at the same time. Until then she didn't know of your existence. The whole thing was altogether too much for her to take. I was away in the Far East and she couldn't contact me for quite a time.'

Holly's brown eyes were soft with sympathy. 'Oh, how awful for her! I *am* sorry.'

His mouth pulled down at the corners. 'She was prostrate on her bed when I got home, filled to the brim with Valium. The doctors had quite a job getting her back on the rails again. I had my hands full with her, too.'

He really did have a most callous way of expressing himself, Holly thought, but she said quietly, 'So perhaps that was why you didn't——'

'Didn't come over for the funeral? Exactly. Did you think it was deliberate?'

Holly said carefully, 'I knew you and Paul weren't on the best of terms.'

He gave a harsh laugh. 'That's putting it mildly! But I would have come if I'd known in time. It was fortunate that Luis Ferida was on the spot—he seemed to manage everything admirably.'

Holly said in a small voice, 'Luis and his sister were wonderfully kind when—when it happened.' Tears pricked behind her eyes as she remembered Juanita's brown eyes full of sympathy, and Juanita's soft arms holding her as she shivered with shock. Luis was the agent in Mexico of Paul's company, and it was at Luis's house that she and Paul had met.

'How is Paul's mother now?' she asked. She had no idea what to expect; Paul had talked very little about his family. She knew he had had letters from his mother, but he had never offered to show them to her, and she never saw him answering any of them.

'She's a wreck, as you'll soon find out. Paul was her darling boy who could do no wrong.' Jared slanted her a glance. 'I'm telling you this so that you'll be able to make up your own mind about how much of the truth to tell her. Or perhaps you may leave her in happy ignorance about the ways of the dear departed.'

Holly stared across the table at the hard, moody face, and was filled with dislike. 'He was your stepbrother,' she said quietly, 'and he's dead. How can you speak like that about him?'

If it were possible his face hardened even more. 'I don't see people through rose-coloured spectacles, dead or alive. I know precisely what kind of a man your late husband was, and so, I should imagine, do you. If you didn't know when you married him it couldn't have taken you long to find out.'

Holly felt sick. Meeting with this man after the long flight, before she had had time to adjust to coming back to England, was taking its toll.

'I don't know what you mean,' she said faintly, fighting down wave after wave of nausea.

His lip curled contemptuously. 'Don't you really? Then you're either ridiculously loyal, or very stupid—or you're lying.'

She stared back unbelievingly into the gunmetal-grey eyes. She was deadly cold and her fingers felt weak and clammy as they wrapped themselves round the coffee beaker.

'Oh, you—you're horrible——' she gasped.

Her eyes dilated and the face of the man and the background of tables and people and lights began to waver and mist over. The beaker slithered from her hand, slopping its contents over the table. There was a roaring noise in her ears.

Dimly she was aware that she was being yanked to the end of the bench seat and her head pushed down between her knees. Everything went on spinning and whirling for what seemed an eternity, but gradually the roaring died away and the pressure on her neck relaxed. She lifted her head slowly and opened her eyes.

'Better?' The man's face was very close to hers; he was kneeling on the floor beside her and the girl in the pink overall hovered behind him, her eyes goggling. Holly looked around and saw that she was the focus of interest for the occupants of all the other tables in the snack-bar.

She sat up slowly, pushing back her hair. The little black pillbox hat had fallen off and was lying on the floor. She picked it up and held it in her hand. 'I—I think so.'

Jared got to his feet. 'You'll be okay when you get outside in the air,' he said brusquely. 'Come along, I'll help you.'

She felt strong arms closing round her and holding her as she tottered out of the room. The cool evening air touched her cheeks and she gulped it in gratefully.

'I'm—all right now.' She tried feebly to draw out of his arms. She didn't want him touching her.

But he didn't relax his hold. 'We'll get you into the car,' he said.

She tried again to wriggle free. 'I can walk,' she said, hoping it was true, for her knees felt like elastic.

'I wouldn't bet on it.' Suddenly he scooped her up and carried her towards the car. She could feel the muscles hardening in his arms as they took her weight.

He was breathing quickly and his breath was hot on her cheek. The softness of her breasts was pressing against the rough material of his safari jacket. She had a brief, terrifying sensation of being overpowered by some force that she was not strong enough to resist and she opened her mouth to scream. But before any sound could come out she was set down beside the car, its long black bonnet sticking out far beyond that of the little Minis on either side.

Jared unlocked the car and opened the passenger door with one hand, keeping his other arm round her. He looked down, 'Okay now?' he said.

She nodded, but he didn't take his arm away. And then a strange thing happened. Just for a moment Holly forgot whose arm was holding her. In a strange sort of way it felt like a shield and protection against the world that had treated her so unkindly in the past months. Weakly she let her head fall to rest against the hard chest of the man beside her, and felt his arm move closer round her waist.

'Good God, there's nothing of you, girl,' he muttered, then, with a jerky movement, he released her and bundled her into the car and slammed the door. Holly huddled into her corner and closed her eyes. She heard the snarl of the engine starting up; the glare of overhead lighting moved whitely across her lids, the engine note changed, settled into its tigerish purr. Then there was nothing but the feel and smell of the car's luxurious leather seating, and the consciousness of the strong male body so close beside her, and again—because she wasn't thinking clearly at all now—there was a sensation of comfort in it.

After a time there was nothing at all. Holly slept.

For what seemed an eternity she slept in snatches,

half-waking to the warmth inside the car and the white beam of headlights probing the darkness ahead. At some time during the journey it started to rain and the windscreen wipers moved monotonously backwards and forwards. Each time she opened her eyes the dazzle of lights from oncoming cars got less and less, until finally there was none at all.

Then at last she was wide awake and there was no sound but the patter of soft rain on the roof of the car. The door on her side was swinging open and a single light shone over the doorway of a long, low white house. They had arrived at Paul's home.

Holly pulled herself stiffly out of the car and stood for a moment holding on to the door-handle to steady herself. Jared was standing at the front door, her bags beside him. He opened the door and light flooded out, illuminating a gravel drive flanked by a wide bed of roses.

He pushed the door open and walked back to the car. 'We're here,' he said. 'come in. There'll probably be some food left out for us. My stepmother will be in bed—no doubt topped up with Mogadons.'

The biting irony in his voice brought Holly abruptly back to full awareness of the situation. Paul was dead. This was his home. The tall, forbidding man grasping her by the elbow and propelling her forward as if she were his prisoner was Paul's stepbrother, the man Paul hated. And somewhere behind the darkened windows Paul's mother lay in a drugged sleep, prostrated by the loss of her only son.

Not a happy situation. Holly felt a shudder of aversion pass through her and shook off the man's hand violently. He let her go without a word and she followed him as he strode through a hall into a long living room, switching on lights as he went.

'Sit here,' he said. 'I'll go and see what Mrs Platt has left for us.'

Holly blinked in the light of a crystal chandelier above her head. 'I don't want anything,' she said faintly. 'I'd like to go straight to bed.'

He shrugged. 'As you please. It's the first room on the left at the top of the stairs. I'll bring your bags up.'

'Thank you.' Somehow she crossed the hall and dragged herself up the stairs, gripping the handrail, drawing in long breaths, willing herself to reach the bedroom. The man was climbing the stairs close behind her and she went icy-cold, in a blind panic.

She staggered up the last stairs, round the corner and into the first room she came to. Jared was close behind her. She felt his arm brush against her as he lifted it to switch on the light, and she recoiled and nearly fell over, bumping into a cane chair and sending it flying.

Jared put her bag on the bed, righted the chair, and stood looking down at her. 'You *are* in a state, aren't you? Jet-lag, no doubt. You'd better get to bed and sleep it off. Bathroom in there.' He nodded towards a door on the other side of the room.

'Thank you,' she said, avoiding his eyes. Get out, she was willing him feverishly. Get *out*, get away from me. The impact of his personality was overwhelming, and the sight of him standing there beside the bed was having a devastating effect on her. Not that he would try anything on, she was sure he wouldn't, but the arrogant masculinity of the man roused an answering feminine response in her body, tired though she was.

'Goodnight,' she said pointedly.

The faintest of crinkles touched the corners of the grey eyes. The brute—did he know what had passed through her mind? But he merely nodded briefly, went out and shut the door.

Holly drew in a great sigh of relief as she sank down on to the bed. All she wanted at the moment was oblivion, and now she could crawl into bed and shut out everything until morning. She hadn't expected this visit to be easy, but she hadn't expected Paul's stepbrother to be quite so beastly to her. She'd been quite wrong about him at the motorway service station, when she'd imagined that he could comfort her. 'Not an ounce of kindness in the man,' she mumbled to herself as she stepped out of her black skirt and let it fall to the floor.

Usually she cared for her clothes lovingly and the black suit had been bought specially when she was all excited about her Mexican trip as David Behrens's P.A. Only a few months ago, but now it seemed in another life that she had been infatuated with David and he had let her down so hurtfully. The suit had cost a week's wages and it had seemed worth it at the time, but tonight she let the skirt lie where it fell. The little black jacket came off next. For a moment it balanced on the back of the cane chair and then slid off on to the carpet, and a moment later her white blouse came to rest on the top of the sad little heap. She let it lie there.

It took quite an effort to get across the room to the adjoining small bathroom, and an even greater effort to get back and struggle with the lock of her travelling case. Defeated finally, and almost weeping with frustration, Holly pushed the case, still firmly locked, on to the floor, repeating parrotlike, 'Not an ounce of kindness,' under her breath, as if it were *his* fault that the lock was stuck.

The bed was soft but exceedingly chilly to her bare
flesh, and it was the first time in her life she had ever
been to bed without washing her face. But she didn't
care about that. She didn't care about anything. 'Not
an ounce of kindness,' she went on muttering, like a
child learning a poem, and she began to giggle with
something near to hysteria.

Then she groaned as she realised she had forgotten
to turn out the light. Forcing herself out of bed again,
she lurched to the doorway and released the switch. In
the sudden darkness she collided with the cane chair
on the way back and it fell over with a protesting
creak. All right—let it stay there. She yawned so
hugely that her jaw hurt as she groped her way back to
the bed and fell into it.

'Not an ounce—' she mouthed as she huddled
beneath the duvet in the blessed darkness, her feet icy
cold.

It seemed like the next second that the light was
switched on again. 'Oh no!' groaned Holly, shielding
her eyes against the blinding whiteness that flooded
the room. She opened them by a sheer effort of will.
Jared Kent was standing by the bed, a mug in one
hand and a red rubber hot water bottle in the other.

He put the steaming mug on the bedside table and
Holly got the unmistakable childhood smell of hot
milk. 'My old nanny said you should never go to bed
on an empty stomach,' he said, and added, 'or in a
cold bed.' He twitched the duvet back quickly and she
felt a stream of chilly air strike her naked body. She
gave a horrified little gasp, grabbed the duvet and
pulled it up to her chin, and she saw his mouth twitch,
but he made no remark, merely held out the hot water
bottle to her. She stuck out a hand and grabbed it and

tucked it down beside her. 'Thank you,' she murmured almost inaudibly.

Jared turned to the door, then he saw the cane chair, lying drunkenly on top of the heap of clothes, and clicked his tongue. 'Tut-tut, Nanny wouldn't have approved of that either.'

Holly's eyes followed him over the top of the duvet in dazed unbelief as he straightened up the chair once again and draped the black suit somewhat clumsily over the back of it. Then he came over and switched on a lamp on the bedside table.

For a moment he stood looking down at her and the light fell on his face, emphasising the hard bone-structure, the straight, unsmiling mouth.

'Drink up your milk,' he said. 'Goodnight.' The ceiling light was switched off and the door closed behind him.

It must have been a dream, Holly thought dazedly. But the hot milk was real enough and the warmth to her chilled feet was quite exquisitely comforting. Before she put out the bedside lamp and snuggled down she had drained the mug.

'Perhaps *half* on ounce of kindness,' she murmured into the darkness before she fell into a deep sleep.

Holly slept soundly and wakened with a clear head, knowing where she was and what had happened last night. The clock on the bedside table told her it was a quarter past nine and her stomach told her she was very, very hungry.

She had no idea what to expect in this house. If Mrs Kent were a semi-invalid at the moment there would presumably be help of some kind—a daily woman, perhaps, or a living-in married couple. Last night that

man had said something about a Mrs Platt, who
sounded like a housekeeper. She slid out of bed,
pulled back the curtains, and opened the door a crack
to listen, but there wasn't a sound of any kind in the
house. She stood looking around. Last night she had
been too exhausted to take in anything but now she
saw that the bedroom was prettily, but rather fussily
furnished. A silky white carpet covered the floor and
wallpaper, bedcovers and curtains all blossomed in
flower-sprigged prints. Ruched white net criss-crossed
over the window. The built-in cupboards had gold
garlands and gold keys.

It was all a little too chi-chi for Holly. This would
be her new mother-in-law's taste, no doubt. From the
little that Paul had told her about his family she had
got the impression of his mother as a pretty, dainty,
rather delicate woman, who had married for the
second time a man many years older than herself, and
that his stepfather had died only a very short time ago.

'She should never have married him,' Paul had
grumbled, 'but we were running out of money, and
you know how it is——?' He had shrugged, fully
expecting her to agree that marrying for money was a
right and reasonable thing to do. 'The old boy carted
us off to live in the middle of nowhere and expected
her to settle down. That was two years ago. I was
absolutely skint at the time and I had to go along too.
God, it was boring! Oh, he did his best, I suppose, he
was generous enough so long as I made some sort of
show at working in his stupid textile mill. It wasn't so
bad until he died. Then I found I was working with
brother Jared, and that was when the rot really set in.
We hated each other's guts from the start, and he did
everything he could to make my life a misery—the

bastard. My mother's too.' Holly stood staring out of the window now at the bleakness of the moors, thinking about Paul's mother. Poor little woman, losing her husband so soon after she had married him, and Paul's death must have been the final blow. Had she known the kind of man her son had grown into? Probably not. Paul hid his true self behind a mask of charm, as she knew to her cost. Everyone thought he was marvellous—until they found out what lay beneath. She had found out, and his brother Jared had found out. That, Holly thought wryly, was the only thing they had in common.

She pulled aside the net curtains, threw open the window, and looked out over a wide, neglected garden with a ragged hedge at the bottom, and beyond that fields and hills, rising eventually to mountains, grey and forbidding. Between the farthest belt of trees the waters of a lake gleamed dully. Rain must have poured down all night and everything was drenched. The smell of wet earth came up through the window, the plaintive bleat of sheep was the only sound. This was a place that could be desolate and threatening if you weren't in the right mood.

Just now she certainly wasn't in the right mood. She turned back to the room, and her eye caught her black suit draped over the back of the cane chair. She felt her body warm with embarrassment as she remembered vividly the episode of the hot water bottle, and she got a mental picture of Jared Kent tossing back the duvet and seeing a white, naked body curled up under it. She giggled. 'That's your reward for the half an ounce of kindness, Mr Jared Kent—if you enjoy that kind of thing.'

She knew from Paul that Jared wasn't married, and now she had met him she guessed that he was the type of man who would attract plenty of women—the kind of women who liked their men tough and primitive. But not her, oh, certainly not her. In spite of the half-ounce of kindness he had shown her somewhat belatedly, she thought she had never met a man whom she so heartily disliked at first sight.

There was one thing she was determined on, and that was that she wasn't going to allow him to walk all over her, as he had tried to do last night. She had learned a lot about men in the last few months and she believed she could hold her own in any sort of confrontation. First David Behrens, then Paul, now this Jared individual. Men, she thought, in spite of their grudging acceptance of women's equality, all they really wanted from women was to bolster their egos and minister to their selfish needs. And Jared Kent struck her as being one of the worst of his kind.

As she showered her mind went back over all that happened in the last few traumatic weeks. It had started when David Behrens asked her to go with him to Mexico to a textile fair, where he was representing the company as its marketing manager.

She had worked as David's secretary for eight months and been in love with him for seven and a half of those months. With his sensational good looks and effortless charm he was so wonderful, so brilliant, so utterly super in every way that it had never occurred to her that he might feel the same way about her and when, one evening after work, he took her out to dinner and suggested that she should go with him on this trip to Mexico she had nearly passed out with rapturous surprise. 'I can't do without you, Holly,' he had said, and his eyes told her more than the words said. 'I need you with me—for good.'

When she had got over the first shock and convinced herself that it was really true Holly hugged herself ecstatically, basked in the envy of her two flatmates, and spent every last penny on clothes to take along with her, and the first few days in Mexico City had been heaven. The work was thrilling too. David was marketing manager for a huge textile firm, one of the biggest in Britain. He had a genius for selling and Holly picked up a great deal by being with him and watching him. She met a lot of people and had the heady excitement of knowing they all liked her. That was when she met Luis Ferida and his sister, Juanita, and it was at a party at Luis's house that she first met Paul.

She remembered that night vividly, remembered the flattery in Paul's eyes, the teasing slant of his mouth. 'You're here with David Behrens, are you?' he had said. 'You want to watch that bloke—ask him where he's parked his wife this time.'

Paul had been fooling, of course. David was going to marry her, he had told her so. He didn't just mean an affair, if he had he would have suggested making love to her before now, and he hadn't. His kisses had been intoxicating, but he hadn't ever taken it further. She thought that was marvellously honourable of him and dreamed constantly of their life together.

She closed her eyes now as she remembered the day when the blow fell. She was responsible for all the book-keeping and she had drawn David's attention to what she had thought of as his mistake in one of the invoice forms he had made out, involving a discrepancy of three thousand pounds. He had laughed—actually laughed—at her. 'Oh, darling girl, you don't want to worry your sweet little head about that. That's one of what's known as perks. There'll be a good many more before we get back to England, you'll see. You'll back me up, like a dear sweet girl, and we'll have a wonderful time together when this trip is over. Until then, we'll watch our steps, yes?'

Holly had wanted to die. David didn't mean to marry her, or even make her his mistress. He had just softened her up to use as a willing accomplice in his dirty-tricks department. Disgusted and sickened, she had said nothing, just booked out of her room at the hotel and left a note for David resigning her job. She had never thought of telling the company what was going on—she didn't think they would have believed her anyway. David Behrens was a top man and she was merely a secretary. They would probably think he had rejected her, and would put it down to pique.

The only person she could turn to was Juanita—Luis Ferida's sister, with whom she had struck up a friendship, and Juanita had been wonderful. She would tell nobody, she promised, not even Luis. Holly must stay with her for a little while. 'You can hide away, so that you cannot be found by that wretch,' she had said, her black eyes flashing. 'I will find out when he has gone from Mexico and then you can come out.'

Juanita had been as good as her word. She was a buyer in one of the big fashion stores in the Zona Rosa—Mexico City's exclusive shopping centre—and had her own beautiful apartment near to Chapultepec Park. After three days she had returned home one evening to announce that the Fair was over and she had made sure that David Behrens had flown back to England. 'You can come out now, Holly,' she had announced. 'And we shall give you a good time to make up. I shall have a party, to start.'

Holly hadn't felt at all like a party, but Juanita had been so kind and understanding that she couldn't refuse.

That was when she had met Paul again.

She had never told Paul the whole story, but he had known David, and she thought he filled in the gaps for himself. He was a lifeline for her.

She needed to go on working, he urged her. How about helping him? He was in the same line of business, she could really be invaluable to him. Holly had been flattered and had jumped at the opportunity. At Juanita's urging she stayed on in her apartment and filled her days with activity, to wipe out the bitter reminders of David.

She didn't see a great deal of Paul after that. He turned up at the apartment now and again and expressed his satisfaction at the work she was doing on his behalf and the contacts she was making—mostly through Juuanita, of course.

Paul had handed over his case to her with all the swatches of the beautiful printed fabrics which his firm in England manufactured, and Holly had not needed to fake her enthusiasm for them. She managed to pass on that enthusiasm to a large garment-making firm, and one day had landed a sizeable order with them. That had been when Paul had asked her to marry him.

As the cool water of the shower tingled on her body the small bathroom with its pink and chrome fittings faded and she was back again in a dark cavern of a restaurant in Mexico City, with the candlelight falling on the dusky smooth shoulders of beautiful women, and the glitter of jewellery, and the smell of exotic food, and a guitar twanging softly and intimately in the shadows.

Paul had been in a euphoric mood that night and delighted with her. 'Clever little darling, aren't you, Holly? How did you manage to land that order? I've been trying them for weeks.' In the dim intimacy of the restaurant he had looked so handsome, so charming, his hair gleaming pure gold, his skin sunkissed, his blue eyes teasing, admiring her.

His fingers had twined with hers on the white tablecloth. 'You know, I could just do with someone like you in my life permanently,' he murmured. 'How about if we got married, pretty Holly, and you did my job for me while I put my feet up?' She had laughed with him at the joke—Paul was never serious for long.

But before the evening was out it was plain that this was one thing that he was serious about—he really was asking her to marry him. 'I mean it, Holly, I need you. You're a lovely, lovely girl and I adore you. We'd make an unbeatable team together. What do you say, darling? Partners?'

The part of her that David had left bruised and raw had started to heal. She had felt loved, protected, successful. And she had had far too much wine to drink over dinner. She smiled hazily into Paul's blue eyes across the table.

A week later they were married.

She was shivering as she stepped from the shower and wrapped herself in a fleecy towel. She mustn't brood on the past now, however much she regretted it. The first thing to be done was to dress and find her way downstairs and see what was happening in the silent house. And the next thing was to find Jared Kent and make it quite clear to him that she intended their contact with each other to be as brief as possible.

She dried her body vigorously until she was glowing

again, remembering how absolutely horrid he had been to her from the first moment she saw him at Heathrow. She couldn't wait to turn her back on him, and this house, to cut the final links that connected her with a most unhappy episode in her life.

CHAPTER TWO

THE locks of her case opened sweetly this morning and Holly took out tan cord pants and a knitted sweater in a rich maize colour, a shade or two darker than her hair. After a quick shower she dressed and brushed her hair and tied it back with a velvet ribbon. She put on the minimum of eye make-up and glossed her lips lightly, then she knotted a brightly patterned scarf round her neck. If that man was still around she didn't intend to lay herself open to any more snide remarks about 'widow's weeds'.

Downstairs in the hall she stood and listened again, but there was no sign of life. The door to the long drawing room was open and a glance told her that it was empty. After the 'prettiness' of the bedroom, this part of the house looked traditional, a comfortable English country home, with Sanderson prints and solid oak everywhere. There were even antlers hanging in the hall above the grandfather clock. She tried two more doors, one that led to a dining room with a long polished table and carved chairs with high backs. Nobody there. Nobody behind the third door either, in what looked like a small study.

It was a pleasant enough house, but everywhere she looked had an uncared-for appearance, as if there would be dust under all the furniture. Evidently Mrs Platt, whoever she was, was taking advantage of the mistress being confined to her bed.

But Holly didn't wait to explore further. She was

feeling quite faint with hunger and she had to find the kitchen. Pushing open a swing door at the back of the hall, she walked to the end of a short passage and found a large kitchen, fitted with modern pine units, facing her. Jared Kent was standing in front of the table. His thick dark hair stood up in spikes as if he had been running his fingers through it. A limp tea-towel drooped from the belt of his tight-fitting brown pants. The sleeves of his khaki shirt were rolled above the elbow, showing strongly-muscled forearms. From the side view she had of his face it looked like a thunder-cloud. He spun round when he heard her come into the kitchen, muttering darkly, 'Blasted woman!'

He must have seen the look of outrage on Holly's face and for the first time she surprised something that might have been a smile touching the corners of his long mouth. 'No, I wasn't referring to you. It's the daily woman, Mrs Platt, she hasn't turned up again. Just look at this place!'

Holly looked. The sink was piled with dirty dishes. The worktops were littered with jars and packets, some of them spilling out their contents. The floor looked as if it needed scrubbing.

'This is the third one who's let me down in a month. Women!' He raised his eyes to the ceiling.

He attacked a loaf of bread with a carving knife, hacked off a slice and then, yanking butter from the fridge, dabbed it in blobs on the bread. He surveyed the result with a groan. 'Blanche won't eat that. Dainty bread and butter arranged on a china plate is what Blanche insists on. Anything else will "turn her stomach".' He mimicked the last words in a high falsetto voice.

Up to this point Holly hadn't said a word, but now she said calmly, 'Is there any marmalade?'

The dark brows went up, but he opened a cupboard and took out a pot of marmalade. 'What's that in aid of?' he growled.

'Well,' said Holly, 'I'm ravenous, and if Blanche—whoever she is—won't eat that slice of bread and butter, I will.' She picked up a knife, spread marmalade thickly and dug her small white teeth into the tempting result with gusto. 'Um, that's good,' she mumbled, and finished off the slice. 'Would you know how to make coffee?'

Jared drew in a long-suffering breath, but set the filter-pot going without a word and in a minute or two the rich aroma spread through the kitchen. By the time it was ready Holly had cut herself two more thick slices of bread and butter and marmalade and consumed the lot.

She pulled a chair up to the table and sat down. 'That's better. I just realised I hadn't eaten for nearly twenty-four hours. Shall I pour the coffee? Have you had your breakfast? And who, by the way, is Blanche?'

He gave her a sour look and sat down at the table opposite her. 'Question one—yes. Question two—no. Question three—Blanche is my stepmother. A silly, helpless little woman, but quite unable to fend for herself at the moment. I can't very well let her starve.' Holly thought his tone suggested that he wouldn't at all mind doing so.

She poured out two cups of coffee and pushed one across the table to him. 'Shouldn't you be at work? You run the mill, don't you?'

'Of course I should be at work,' he barked. 'And I do run the mill—when I manage to get there. But if there are many more domestic crises demanding my attention,' he went on with heavy irony, 'there won't be any mill to run.'

Holly cut two more slices of bread and butter, put them on a plate and pushed it across the table to him. 'There you are, then,' she said, 'that will keep you going for an hour or two. After you've eaten that I suggest you take yourself off and leave me to cope. Men!' She raised her eyes to the ceiling in a fair imitation of the way he had done himself only a couple of minutes ago.

The moody grey eyes fixed themselves doubtfully upon hers, as if he suspected her of double dealing of some kind. 'Are you serious?' he said. 'You don't know——'

'Look, Mr Jared Kent,' Holly interrupted him, 'I'm perfectly serious. I'm not silly and I'm not weak and I'm quite capable of finding my way around here for the *very* short time I intend to stay. If I can be of any use to Paul's mother in that time I'm ready to do what I can. But I'm sure I shall manage much better without your help. Without any man's help, if it comes to that.'

He stood up, glaring down at her darkly as she sat at the table calmly drinking her coffee. 'We have a feminist in our midst, have we?' he said nastily.

Holly shrugged. 'Not particularly. I don't go for putting people into boxes. Now, hadn't you better be getting along?'

She saw the sudden flash of anger that came into the steely grey eyes, and felt again that grip of something like fear in the pit of her stomach. He could be a dangerous man if roused, she was sure of that, and she wondered if she had been too ready to cross swords with him.

He walked round the table and stood behind her chair and for a moment she felt the weight of his hand on her shoulder. 'Don't go too far, my girl,' he said softly. 'I don't take kindly to being baited.' His anger reached her through the touch of his fingers and she felt a quiver pass through her.

He walked to the door. 'We'll talk when I get home,' he said, and went out of the kitchen. A moment later she heard the roar of a car engine die away down the road.

Holly sat very still. 'Beast,' she said aloud. 'Bully!' Well, we know where we stand with each other now. Armed combat, that was the name of the game for as long as she was here.

She would find Paul's mother and do what she could to help her. That was what she had come for, not to fight with his beastly brother. She owed this family nothing, she told herself, she had only come here out of a sense of compassion for Mrs Kent, and there was no need for her to put up with the kind of treatment she had received from Jared.

I'll leave tomorrow, she told herself. Nothing will make me stay longer than that.

She rubbed her shoulder where Jared Kent's strong fingers had dug into it. 'Nothing,' she repeated firmly, aloud.

After a moment or two she stood up, still dithering a bit inside after that brush with Jared. The man got right under her skin, she admitted to herself. She must get busy and put him out of her mind entirely. The first thing to do was to find her unknown mother-in-law and introduce herself. The best way would seem to be to take a breakfast tray up to her. If she could appear bearing the dainty fare which that lady appreciated it might help to break the ice.

It didn't take long. In a very few minutes a tray was set with a lacy cloth, a plate of thin bread and butter, jars of marmalade and honey, tea in a blue china pot and milk in a cream jug to match. Holly regarded it with satisfaction. That should be dainty enough for anyone.

At the top of the stairs she paused, looking around. Which room? The one to the left was where she had slept last night. She pushed open the door of the next room and saw a rumpled bed, a pair of moccasins thrown down into it, and a heap of garments on the floor, presumably waiting to be washed. Jackets hung crazily on the backs of chairs, shoes were scattered beneath. Jared's bedroom, obviously. Nanny would quite definitely *not* have approved! Well, *she* was certainly not going to do anything about it. The very thought of going into the man's bedroom stirred her inside up again in an odd way, and she shut the door quickly.

There was a passage next, with several doors leading off it, and she tried the first one. She knew as soon as she opened the door that this was Mrs Kent's bedroom. The curtains were drawn across the window and an electric fire was making the room stuffy. Holly could see the outline of a large bed in the far corner of the room, and in it a hump of bedclothes. Paul's mother, she supposed.

The hump stirred slightly. 'Is that you, Mrs Platt?' A high little-girl voice came from the direction of the bed.

Holly moved forward. 'It isn't Mrs Platt,' she said. 'Shall I draw back the curtains?' She didn't wait for an answer. She pulled back the long velvet curtains and the morning light streamed into the room. At a glance

Holly saw that this room had been completely made over. It looked like a bedroom from *Ideal Home*. All in white, built-in fitments up to the ceiling, mirrors everywhere, an inches-thick carpet.

A face emerged above the white satin bed-cover, wincing against the light. Holly had vaguely imagined her mother-in-law as middle-aged, grey-haired, a bit plump, perhaps. The face that she saw could hardly have been less like her picture. But what gave her a sudden twist inside was the extraordinary likeness to Paul. The same bubbling curls of corn-coloured hair, damp now and straggly; the same golden skin; the same blue eyes with their wide, ingenuous expression, dulled now by the tranquillisers she had been taking.

Holly did a quick calculation. Paul had been twenty-five, so his mother must be over forty, but she looked ten years younger—or she could do if she made an effort about her appearance. She pulled herself up in the bed now, blinking at Holly. 'Who are you? Where's Jared? He said he would come home last night. I've been all alone. I didn't know what was going on.' She passed a small delicate hand confusedly across her eyes.

Holly stood beside the bed. 'I'm Holly,' she said. 'I've brought you some breakfast, Mrs Kent.'

The smooth, childish forehead puckered. 'Holly? Then where's Mrs Platt? What's happening? I don't understand.'

Holly went out to the landing, brought the tray in and set it beside the bed. Before she said anything more she poured a cup of tea and put it into the hands of the woman in the bed, who sipped it slowly, her wide blue eyes fixed on Holly.

When she had drunk it all Holly took the cup and

replaced it on the tray. 'Mrs Platt hasn't turned up this morning,' she said matter-of-factly. 'Jared has gone out to the mill. And I've come to see you and——' she hesitated, not quite knowing how to put this '——and talk to you about Paul.'

'Then—then you're——'

'Paul's wife—yes,' Holly said.

'Oh!' She saw realization dawn in the blue eyes. Then the pretty childish face crumpled up as Paul's mother buried it in the pillow and began to sob uncontrollably.

It was an emotional half-hour that followed. Holly did her best, but it wasn't easy to cope. Blanche Kent was a type she hadn't encountered before, a woman who almost seemed to enjoy pouring out her grief. Between her sobs she drew a picture of Paul that Holly hardly recognised. He was a wonderful, wonderful son, whose one aim in life was to care for his mother. Unselfish, generous, thoughtful. Everything, it seemed to Holly, that Paul certainly was *not*. But she didn't demur. She sat on the edge of the bed and listened, nodding now and again, which was all that seemed required of her.

At last Blanche dabbed her eyes and seemed to notice Holly's presence. 'So—he married you, did he? That was why he didn't write to me, was it? I suppose he didn't want to hurt me.'

Holly said gently, 'Why should it hurt you, Mrs Kent?'

Blanche Kent wiped her eyes on a wisp of handkerchief. 'Of course it would hurt me, not knowing,' she said tremulously. 'He always told me everything.'

'I think he wanted to surprise you,' Holly improvised, and was rewarded by a watery smile.

'Yes, that would be like Paul,' his mother sighed. 'He loved to play jokes. When he was a little boy he was always thinking up something to surprise me.' Her mouth quivered again. 'But now he's dead and he was all I had, and now I'm quite alone in this great cold house.'

She looked as if she might relapse into tears again, and Holly hastily put the tray on her knees. 'Look, have some breakfast, Mrs Kent. I'm sure you'll feel better when you've eaten something.'

Blanche eyed the daintily-arranged tray. 'Well, perhaps I should,' she said reluctantly. 'The doctor says I must keep up my strength.'

'Quite right,' Holly agreed. 'I'll pour you another cup of tea.'

Blanche ate up every bit of the bread and butter. Then she lay back against the lace-trimmed pillows and sighed. 'Thank you, that was very nice, Holly. I do like thin bread and butter, but nobody here seems to know how to cut it. The woman we have at present is dreadful—so rough and uncouth.' She shuddered. 'I wanted to get rid of her, but Jared wouldn't have it. He's so—so dominating, he just goes his own way, whatever I say or think, not like his father—my dear husband, who was so kind and generous.' Her lips trembled. 'Jared is my stepson. Have you seen him since you arrived?'

'He met my plane in London yesterday and drove me up here,' said Holly, in some surprise. Was Blanche Kelly really so out of touch with what was going on in the house?

'Oh yes, I think he told me.' Again the hand passed across the white forehead. 'I get so muddled at present, you know. I simply can't pull myself together.

There's been nobody—nobody to help me. Nobody to talk to.' A small sad smile touched the pretty mouth. 'But now you're here, Holly, I shall be much, much better, I'm sure of it. I won't need these any longer.' She picked up a bottle of tablets on the bedside table, and looked wryly at it and then at Holly. 'You know, my dear, there have been times lately when I've been tempted to——' She shook the bottle and the tablets rattled inside.

'Oh *no*, no, you mustn't,' Holly said quickly. 'You mustn't even think of it. You can have a wonderful life before you. You're young and—and so pretty.' That sounded a bit fulsome, but it was the plain truth. Blanche could be very pretty indeed if she took a little trouble with herself. She smiled a watery smile. 'That's sweet of you, Holly, do you really think so?'

'Of course I do.' Holly stood up. 'Now, I'd better go downstairs and tidy things up. It seems that the woman hasn't turned up this morning and Jared has gone out to his mill.'

Blanche pulled a face. 'That's all the man thinks of—the mill, and making money. His father wasn't like that at all, and *he* made a wonderful success of the firm, *he* didn't find it necessary to spend every hour of the day at the mill. He was always ready to take me out and invite friends here. A real open house it was—we had such fun.' She sighed heavily. 'And Paul was always happy to be here with me. But when my husband died last year everything changed. That son of his changed it all. He's so cold, so hard.' She shivered. 'I can't do with men like that.'

Holly stood holding the tray. She had heard all this before—from Paul. And from what she had seen of Jared Kent she was inclined to believe it. Cold—

hard—yes, that was the picture he presented. For a moment last night she thought she might have misjudged him, but now she decided that the warm milk and the hot water bottle were merely insurances against the unwelcome visitor—herself—becoming chilled and getting ill. No doubt he was as anxious to get rid of her as she was to get away from this unwelcoming house.

'You'll have to tell me what you'd like me to do for you today,' she said. 'As the woman hasn't come I could do a bit of cooking for you while I'm here. Will you be getting up now, Mrs Kent?'

Blanche drew further into the bed, looking alarmed. 'I—I don't know if I'm strong enough yet.' She brightened. 'The doctor will probably be calling this morning, so I think I'll stay in bed for a while.' She put out a small, weak hand and clasped Holly's arm. 'Do make yourself at home, my dear—and please don't call me Mrs Kent. Everyone calls me Blanche.' She smiled winningly, and Holly felt a strange sense of having seen that smile before. Paul had smiled just like that when he wanted something from her. She felt sorry for this pathetic little woman, but she mustn't allow Paul's mother to lean on her in the way that Paul had done. I'll leave tomorrow, she told herself again as she carried the tray downstairs.

Back in the kitchen she washed the dishes and cleaned the sink. Then she looked in the fridge to see what there was in stock, and wasn't encouraged by what she found. Eggs, butter, milk, the remains of a pie with a very thick, pale crust, a large piece of yellow cheese, covered with fuzzy green mould, and in the freezer compartment an assortment of packets of frozen meat and fish and a bag of peas. Who did the

shopping around here? she wondered. The absent Mrs
Platt? Or that male chauvinist man of the house?
Certainly not Blanche Kent, in her present condition.
Well, it was no business of hers, she didn't owe this
family anything, and she would only be here a few
hours longer.

A faint sound from the direction of the window
made her turn quickly, to see the face of a black and
white cat pressed against the wet pane, its mouth wide
open in an anguished howl. Another member of the
family demanding food, evidently! Holly opened the
window and the cat jumped in and immediately slunk
under the table, eyeing her with a wide, pale-green
stare. It was very wet and it had a battle-scar on one
ear. 'You *are* a poor, miserable-looking animal,' Holly
told it. Either it was a stray, or else nobody had
bothered to feed it for a long time. She crumbled half
a slice of bread into a saucer of milk and placed it in
front of the cat, who applied itself ravenously to the
task of cleaning up the saucer in the shortest possible
time. 'More?' Holly asked it, half amused, half pitying.
It was no beauty, it would never have won a prize in a
show. White markings were splashed haphazardly over
its black coat. Its black legs looked as if they were
wearing four little white boots. It was very thin and
very hungry. A second saucerful went the way of the
first and a third followed, after which the cat emerged
from under the table and began to clean itself.

Holly knelt down beside it and stroked its soft chest,
and was promptly included in the washing process, its
rough little tongue scratching over her fingers, while
its thin stomach vibrated with a loud purr. Holly
smiled slowly. It didn't take much to make a small
animal happy.

There was a noise outside and the back door swung open to admit a woman in a wet mackintosh. She stopped short, eyeing Holly suspiciously. 'Who are you? What are you doing here?'

Holly stood up. 'I'm Holly Ward, Mrs Kent's daughter-in-law. You're Mrs Platt, are you?'

'That's right.' The woman took off her mackintosh, shook it and hung it up behind the door. She was thin and raw-boned, with patches of red veins on her cheeks, lank brown hair and a petulant expression. She turned to the sink. 'You done the washing up?' It sounded like an accusation.

'We thought you might not be coming, Mrs Platt, so I got on with it,' Holly said pleasantly. She didn't like the look of the woman, but it would serve no purpose to get on the wrong side of her.

Mrs Platt opened a cupboard under the sink, clattered in the pans that Holly had washed and slammed the door. 'Can't help me bike getting a puncture, can I?' she demanded truculently. 'Expects me on the dot, her ladyship upstairs does. Wants to be waited on hand and foot.'

'Mrs Kent isn't very well,' Holly said mildly.

The woman stood with hands on hips, mouth dragged down. 'That's a good story, that is. An excuse for lying in bed all day, if you ask me!'

Annoyance and dislike was beginning to simmer inside Holly, but she kept her voice polite as she suggested, 'Well, as you are here now, hadn't you better get on with it?'

Mrs Platt tossed her head. 'Don't you start giving me orders, young woman!' she bridled. 'I'm as good as you are any day, and I don't take orders from the likes of you, I can tell you!' An ugly flush stained the veined cheekbones. She had evidently arrived spoiling for a fight.

At that moment there was a faint mew and the black and white cat slid out from beneath the table. 'That blasted cat again!' Mrs Platt's lips set in an ugly line. 'I won't have it in my kitchen, stealing. Get out, you thieving brute—get out, I say!' She landed a vicious kick at the cat, catching it on its thin stomach, and it let out a banshee wail and fled through the door into the hall.

Holly was appalled. 'How *dare* you kick an animal!' She was breathing fast keeping a tight grip on her overwhelming desire to hit the woman with the first weapon that came to hand.

Mrs Platt's bony nose went up. 'Hoity-toity, that's how it is, is it? Well, I don't think as you and me are going to get on together, *Missus* whatever your name is.'

'I'm heartily in agreement with you,' Holly said icily. 'And while we're on the subject, you can go now, and don't come back.'

For a moment she thought the woman was going to explode. Then she thought better of it. 'Suits me.' She tossed her head. 'But I'm not going from here without me money owing to me.' She planted her feet apart on the tiled floor. 'Four pounds fifty for the two hours.'

Holly restrained her annoyance somehow and went upstairs to get her handbag. She put the money on the table and watched Mrs Platt as she counted it and stuffed it into a capacious purse which she extracted from a carrier bag. Then the woman got herself back into her mackintosh and stamped out of the kitchen without another word. A moment later she passed the window, wheeling her bicycle, umbrage in every line of her body.

Holly slumped into a chair. What had she been thinking of—taking the responsibility of sacking the only person who seemed to stand between this household and utter chaos? She felt something move and saw that the little cat had returned and was rubbing his skinny body against her leg. She picked him up and held him against her cheek, and he began to purr ecstatically. 'What's your name?' said Holly. 'I don't suppose anyone bothered to give you a name, you poor waif.' She stroked his little white boots. 'I shall call you Paws. And what on earth am I going to do with you?'

Perhaps, she thought a little wildly, she could put the cat in a basket and take him with her when she left. Certainly there was nobody here to look after it. But where would she go when she got back to London? She had finally left her flat when she went to Mexico with David Behrens, and they wouldn't take a cat in a hotel, would they?

She glanced at her watch and saw that it was a quarter to twelve. What to do now? She supposed she had better prepare some kind of dainty lunch for Mrs—for Blanche. 'I'll give her a treat, just for today, Paws,' she told the little cat. 'But tomorrow she'll have to fend for herself. And would she remember to feed you, I wonder, if I left you here?' She lifted the cat and hugged it against her, and it lifted one paw and placed it delicately against her cheek. Holly groaned. 'I seem to have a talent for letting people wheedle me,' she said. 'And now—cats! I must kick the habit.' She put the cat down on the floor firmly.

At that moment she heard a car pull up outside the front door. Jared? Her heart started to thump uncomfortably; that man spelled trouble. She braced herself. She would meet him on his own ground and if he wanted a fight he should have it. Although why he should want to fight her she couldn't imagine.

The kitchen door swung open and he stood there, tall and broad and arrogant, and devastatingly good-looking in his tight-fitting dark pants and thin khaki shirt, the sleeves rolled up above the elbows. To her dismay Holly felt a physical surge of man-woman awareness shoot through her. Well, he *was* a very masculine man, he exuded sex-appeal without even trying, but she certainly wasn't going to let that cloud her judgment of him. She said coolly, 'Hullo, you're back soon. I thought you'd gone for the day.'

He strolled across the kitchen and stood by the table, looking down at her. His lashes, she saw at close quarters, were amazingly thick and long and curved at the tips, giving the impression that he was smiling. But he certainly wasn't at the moment.

'I've taken an hour off,' he said shortly. 'We must get things settled, and the sooner the better.'

'What is there to settle?' Holly got to her feet. Her head only reached to his chin, but for some reason she felt more secure standing up. 'I've seen Paul's mother and we've had a talk. I don't think there's much more I can do for her. She's not really ill, is she, and I'm sure if she got up and occupied herself she wouldn't need all those tranquillisers.'

He said drily, 'Too true. And how do you persuade her to get up? I'm damned if I can.'

'I expect you bullied her,' said Holly, looking up at him speculatively. She had a feeling that this interview was going to develop into a battle, and if so it would be useful to get in the first shot.

He glared at her as if he couldn't believe his ears.

Then his eyes went to the floor, where Paws had come from under the table again and was weaving against Holly's legs, mewing hopefully.

'How did that thing get in here?' he demanded. 'It probably belongs to the farm across the valley.'

'Well, if it does they shouldn't be allowed to keep a cat,' Holly said indignantly. 'The poor little thing is almost starving—just look at him!'

His eyes moved accusingly to the empty saucer on the floor. 'And you've been feeding it, you stupid girl?' he roared. 'Now we'll never get rid of the bloody thing. Just one more problem!'

Holly drew in a breath. Better get it all over at once. 'Oh, and by the way, I'm afraid you've lost your Mrs Platt. She's left in a huff.'

'Left? What do you mean—left?' He strode to the window and looked out as if Mrs Platt were lurking there. Then he turned on her. 'Do you mean left for good?'

'I'm afraid so,' Holly said calmly. 'Unlike the cat, she didn't seem to take to me.'

He advanced towards her, and in spite of her resolution to give as good as she got, Holly took a step backwards. His steely grey eyes were glinting with pure rage as he said very softly between his teeth. 'Do you realize that Mrs Platt was all that stood between me and complete insanity? What the hell did you do to make her leave?'

She forced herself to meet his accusing gaze and hoped he couldn't guess how her inside was churning. 'It wasn't what I did, exactly,' she said. 'It was what she did. She kicked Paws. I couldn't let that go, could I?'

'Kicked what?' he shouted. 'Good God, talk sense, girl!'

'Paws,' Holly explained patiently, stooping down and lifting up the cat's two front legs with their little white boots. 'I've called him Paws, he had to have a name. He won't bother you, I promise, I'll take him with me when I leave tomorrow.'

Jared Kent ran his fingers through his rough, dark hair, the picture of a man at the end of his tether. 'Give me strength,' he muttered. Then his eyes narrowed, and again those fantastic lashes gave the impression of a smile. Nothing could have been further from the truth. 'So,' he snarled, 'you got on the wrong side of Mrs Platt and she left, did she? Well, you'll bloody well go into the town and apologise and get her to come back. I can't go on here alone, with that woman lying in bed upstairs expecting to be waited on—and nobody to look after the house——' he punctuated each phrase with a stabbing fingers '—and a thousand and one matters at the mill demanding my attention. Come on.' He grasped her arm. 'We'll go together and explain to Mrs Platt that it was a misunderstanding.' He started to yank her towards the door.

'Let me go!' Holly shouted. 'How dare you touch me?' She resisted with every bit of her strength as he pulled. 'Let me *go*, you great bully!'

'Not on your life!' he shouted back. He had lost his temper completely now and was using all his considerable male strength to force his will on her.

'No—no—*no!*' she yelled, straining away, just as furious as he was. But he was gaining ground and they were nearly at the back door now. Wild with rage Holly lowered her head and sank her teeth into his wrist, biting as hard as she could.

He dropped her arm at once. 'Why, you little hellcat! Why did you do that?' He stared down at his wrist as if he couldn't believe his eyes. 'Now I've had the lot from the women in this house. Not only do they disrupt my life in every possible way, but they attack me like wild animals!'

Holly was gripping the edge of the table, looking a little pale. 'You asked for it,' she said defiantly. 'You shouldn't have used force on me. I don't take that from any man!' She looked down at his wrist. The marks of her teeth were visible, faintly pink against the darker colour of his skin, but there was no sign of blood. He was tough, all right. It would take a lot to pierce his thick hide, she thought disgustedly.

His expression changed and he looked at her rather curiously. Perhaps the shock had calmed him, and just as well too.

'Sit down,' he said.

Holly remained standing, one hand gripping the table.

'Sit down, girl,' he said impatiently. 'The fight's over—for the moment anyway. I've got to talk to you.'

He slumped into one of the kitchen chairs beside the table and Holly took the other one, eyeing him warily. She couldn't quite believe that the fight would ever be over while the two of them were together.

He was in no hurry to talk, he seemed to be deep in thought, his eyes narrowed behind those fantastic lashes. Then abruptly he lifted his head. 'Why did you marry him?' He shot the question at her.

Her mouth opened in surprise. 'I—I——' she stammered, her mind racing. Why *had* she married Paul? It had seemed simple at the time, but now it seemed horribly complicated. She pulled her thoughts together. 'Because I fell in love with him, of course,' she said, lifting her chin a fraction.

He nodded, as if he knew already what she was going to say, and didn't believe a word of it. Then he said grimly, 'And how long did it take you to find out the kind of man he was? A layabout, as selfish as they're made, and a near-alcoholic into the bargain?'

'Oh!' Holly gasped. Put crudely like that it sounded so unnecessarily brutal. 'He's dead,' she whispered. 'You shouldn't——' But already her defences were down as she remembered those awful months when she had been Paul's wife, and that last scene before he had slammed out of the hotel room, already drunk at five o'clock in the afternoon, and lurched out into the chaos of Mexico City's traffic, straight into the path of a lorry. 'Please don't——' Tears forced themselves under her closed eyelids. She had tried so hard to pretend that none of it had ever happened, and now this man was reminding her brutally, and she started to shiver all over.

She wiped her eyes, getting control of herself again, and looked at Jared Kent with dislike. 'Why are you talking to me like this?' she demanded, her voice shaking. 'What good is it doing you? I'm nothing to you—I shall leave here tomorrow. *And* I'll take Paws with me,' she added recklessly, as the little cat jumped up on her knee and began to knead her cord trousers, prior to settling himself down to sleep.

'Believe me, there's nothing that would please me more,' he said nastily, 'but unfortunately, it's impossible. There are things to be settled before you can leave.'

'I've nothing I want to settle with you——' Holly began, 'and the sooner we——'

'Oh, shut up,' he snapped, 'and listen to me. The facts are straightforward enough. So far as I can find out Paul left no will, so you, as his widow, will inherit everything he owned.'

'Oh!' said Holly blankly. 'I never thought of that.'

'Didn't you indeed?' There was no mistaking the sneer in his voice. 'Well, we'll let that go for the moment. What concerns me is that Paul's inheritance happens to be a share of the family business. That woman Blanche could twist my father round her little finger. She persuaded him to alter his will so that her precious son would be amply provided for.'

He was watching her face closely while he spoke. 'Paul didn't tell you? Where did you think the money came from that he spent so freely?'

She shook her head dumbly. Paul had always demanded the best of everything—and got it. The best hotel room, the best food, the best drink. Most of all the best drink. 'I never thought about it,' she whispered.

'Well, think about it now,' Jared said curtly, getting to his feet. 'I shall buy out your share of the business, of course, but that will take time. I'm afraid you can't expect to be a rich widow straight away,' he added, his hard mouth twisting in contempt.

'You—you're insulting, disgusting——' Holly couldn't think of anything bad enough for him. 'I hate you!' she flung at him.

He ignored that and went on as if she hadn't spoken. 'You'll have to see our solicitor. He has an office in Windermere, and I've made an appointment for you for two o'clock this afternoon. I'll be back at a quarter to two to drive you there.'

He walked to the door and then paused, looking around the untidy kitchen. 'Meanwhile,' he added caustically, 'as you've taken it upon yourself to get rid of our only help in the house the least you can do is to attend to the domestic chores yourself for the moment. See you.' He went out and slammed the door smartly behind him.

Holly sat staring at the closed door, her eyes wide with rage. 'Beast!' she fumed, slamming her hand down on the wooden table to emphasize the words. 'Rude, arrogant, boorish——'

The little cat stirred on her knee, stretched, and mewed.

'Oh, not you, my sweet,' said Holly. 'Not you—*him.*'

And into that one small word she managed to put all her pent-up anger and disgust with the male sex in general—and Jared Kent in particular.

CHAPTER THREE

JARED returned at precisely a quarter to two, and Holly was ready and waiting for him. In the interval she had attended to the domestic chores as he had so bitingly suggested—not, she was careful to assure herself, because she had any intention of tamely obeying him, but because it seemed the obvious thing to do and it would be childish to be defensive about it.

She had tidied the kitchen and swept the floor, flicked round the drawing room with a duster, plumped up the cushions and thrown away the faded flowers. Then she prepared a dainty luncheon tray for Blanche, with scrambled eggs, thin bread and butter once again, and coffee with a couple of bourbon biscuits that she had found in a tin and which seemed reasonably fresh.

Blanche had perked up quite considerably since this morning. The doctor had not called, but when Holly suggested that she should get up for tea she hadn't turned down the idea out of hand.

'I have to go to see the solicitor this afternoon,' Holly explained. 'Jared is taking me there, and when I've finished I'll buy some cakes and something for dinner. We could have tea together downstairs when I get back—how would that be?'

Blanche actually smiled. 'I might just manage it.' She eyed the luncheon tray with pleasure. 'This looks really appetising. When I've had lunch I'll have a little rest, then I'll have my bath and see how I feel afterwards.'

'That's marvellous,' Holly encouraged her. 'Now I'd better get ready to go into the town. I can't go like this.' She glanced down at her cords and sweater and pulled a wry face.

The older woman nodded and sighed and put a delicate hand on Holly's arm. There were tears in her eyes. 'You can't guess how glad I am to have you here, my dear,' she said chokily. 'You bring the house to life. I feel better already, and I'm not going to take any more of those tablets.'

'That's splendid,' said Holly, feeling guilty. She ought to tell Blanche straight away that she didn't intend to stay beyond tomorrow, but she couldn't bring herself to do it.

In the bedroom she rummaged in one of her big cases for something to wear. She had given up her share in the London flat when she left for Mexico with David Behrens, and these two cases held all her worldly belongings. None of her clothes seemed particularly suitable for this place, and all of them reminded her of some part of her immediate past that she wanted to forget. When I get back to London I'll give the lot to Oxfam, she vowed, and buy a new wardrobe at Marks and Sparks. Finally she chose a tailored silk two-piece in a deep cream colour with a wide belt, that she had bought in the Zona Rosa in Mexico City, for her wedding to Paul. She fastened the belt and had to pull it in two notches. She must have lost pounds and pounds in the last few weeks. Suddenly she remembered Jared Kent's deep voice, last night, saying, 'There's nothing of you, girl.' He had sounded almost human at that moment, but he'd certainly made up for it today.

When she was ready she looked at herself in the

mirror. She had brushed her hair up into a smooth knot, which made her face look even thinner and paler. She wouldn't let that man think she was making a bid for sympathy, she vowed, flicking blusher on her cheekbones, shading down to the hollows beneath. Not too much lipstick, that made her look worse. You're like an orphan of the storm, she told her reflection with a grimace, but you'll have to do.

Downstairs in the kitchen she ate a couple of biscuits and finished up the coffee she had made for Blanche. Then she went and stood by the front door to wait. From here she could get a view over the shrubs that lined the drive, to the fells beyond—mile after mile of grass and rocks, rising finally to a magnificent range of mountains which receded into the distance, their cover of bracken, beginning to turn red, blazing out against the yellowish grass and the darker green of the trees. Here and there the sunlight glittered on streams that cascaded down, turning them to silver. The rain had stopped and puffy little white clouds scudded busily across the picture-postcard blue of the sky. The air that touched Holly's cheeks was pure and clean. She drew in a deep breath, remembering the smog and pollution of Mexico City as a bad dream.

For the very first time she thought how good it would have been if things had been different here—if Jared Kent had been friendly instead of bitterly antagonistic. She might have stayed for a time and helped Blanche over her depression. She might have come for a visit now and again and drunk in the peace and quiet of this place when London got too much for her. She might even have felt that she had a kind of family.

There was a roar and a swirl of gravel and the big

black car pulled up outside the door. Jared didn't bother to get out, he rolled down the window and called abruptly, 'Ready?'

As the car turned out of the drive and into the lane, the full sweep of the landscape spread out before them. She would have one more try, Holly thought, and said, 'I've been admiring the view. I've never been to the Lakes before and I didn't know how spectacular it is.'

He kept his eyes on the road ahead. 'I'm glad that our scenery, at least, meets with your approval,' he said curtly.

She glanced up at him. Was he joking? Some men used irony as a spice to liven up a conversation. But his profile was as grim and hard as ever. All right, all right, *be* like that, Holly told him silently. I don't care.

They didn't speak again until they reached the town.

Holly wasn't in the mood to notice much about her surroundings as Jared parked the car and led the way into the main street. She was conscious of the mountains brooding over everything, and the blue-grey ruffled water of the lake, glimpsed between the buildings, and the busy streets of the small town, but she was fuming inside with helpless anger and didn't register more than that. The man walking beside her in stony silence was having a devastating effect on her. At the solicitor's office they were greeted by a girl receptionist, who flashed Jared a film-star smile from under heavily mascarawed lashes and led them up a spiral staircase to a first-floor room overlooking the shopping street.

An elderly man came from behind the desk and Jared shook hands with him and introduced Holly, staying near to the door himself. 'I'll leave you to put Mrs Ward into the general picture, as we arranged this morning, Mr Windrush.' He glanced in Holly's direction and added briefly, 'I shan't be able to drive you back, but Mr Windrush will tell you where you can pick up a taxi, so you can make your own way.'

She didn't think that was worth answering, so she said nothing, and, with a nod to the solicitor, Jared left them together. Holly let out a deep breath as the door closed behind him, sinking into the chair that the solicitor drew out for her, feeling as if she had been running a marathon race.

Mr Windrush looked as much a fixture in the office as his wide desk with its untidy piles of papers and the enormous legal tomes that filled the bookshelves. He had thinning grey hair and his ferocious bushy black eyebrows, and half-moon spectacles, gave him an intimidating appearance. Holly's heart sank. What had Jared told him about her, and was he going to bully her too? She didn't think she could take much more.

But when he had settled in his chair the eyes that met Holly's across the wide desk were kind, and when he said, 'Please accept my sincere sympathy in your loss, Mrs Ward. You've been through a painful time,' he spoke as if he really meant it.

'Thank you,' said Holly. Mr Windrush had no doubt been the family solicitor for years and he would know all about Paul, so there was no need for pretence between them.

'Now——' the solicitor pulled a heavy sheaf of documents towards him, 'I understand that Mr Kent has already sketched in the position to you, Mrs Ward? Your husband appears to have died intestate——' he looked keenly at her over the top of his

half-moon spectacles '—leaving no will, you understand, which means that everything he owns will come
to you, as his widow.'

Holly nodded, and Mr Windrush asked her for her
marriage certificate and then droned on about letters
of administration and all the other matters which
would need attention. Holly did her best to follow, but
she was soon lost in the legal terms, and when he said,
'I have the necessary documents ready for your
signature,' she signed where he told her, making only
a pretence at reading them. Finally Mr Windrush sat
back in his chair. 'Mr Jared Kent tells me that he
intends to buy out your share of the business as soon
as poosible.' He looked closely across the desk at her
as if weighing her up. 'Did he explain to you, I
wonder, exactly what that would entail?'

'He didn't explain anything. He merely informed
me what he meant to do.'

'And you agreed?'

'He didn't wait for me to agree.'

'Ah!' Mr Windrush pursed his lips and nodded his
head up and down. No doubt he had Jared Kent
weighed up too.

'Well, Mrs Ward,' he said, 'if Mr Kent didn't make
the situation clear to you, then I must. You have no
idea what your share of the company will be, and the
sum of money involved?'

'No, none at all.' Holly was beginning to be
puzzled. Mr Windrush seemed to be making a big
thing of all this, but surely Paul's share couldn't be so
very large? He had been no blood relative of his
stepfather's, and couldn't have expected to be
remembered all that generously in his will.

Mr Windrush had gone off on another tack. 'I'll

speak frankly to you, Mrs Ward. At the time of his second marriage I tried to dissuade Mr Kent Senior, as his legal adviser, from the course he was taking when he made his new will.' He sighed. 'But he was adamant. You see, as so often happens with a late marriage, he was very much in love with his pretty, much younger, wife. His first wife had been dead for many years and I believe he had a—er—somewhat sentimental dream of a family all living together in perfect amity, and the two sons working in harness. He wanted everything to be shared equally between them—no favouritism, you understand. Unfortunately——' he pulled a wry face '—human nature being what it is, things didn't work out quite like that, and after his death there was a good deal of bad feeling. It was inevitable, I fear. The family business was started a hundred years ago and has been handed down from father to son ever since. To bring a stranger in, as he did, was asking for trouble.'

Mr Windrush cleared his throat and added apologetically, 'I mention this, Mrs Ward, because it has some bearing, I believe, on the present situation. Of course, Mr Kent Senior was a very rich man. The house belongs to his son Jared, but Mrs Kent inherited a capital sum which provides her with a handsome income. The family textile business was willed equally between his son Jared and his stepson Paul. Paul's share now devolves to you, Mrs Ward, as his widow.' He paused and then added impressively, 'A half-share in Kent and Son.'

'A *half*-share?' Holly's eyes flew open wide. 'Are you quite sure?' she added. How stupid—of course a solicitor would be sure.

'Quite sure,' said Mr Windrush dryly. 'If Mr Jared

Kent buys you out, as he proposes, there will be a very large capital sum to come to you.'

Holly's hands closed on the wooden arms of her chair. She said faintly, 'How—how much?'

The solicitor placed his fingers together. 'At this stage it is impossible to say precisely, but I recall the valuation on the death of Mr Kent Senior a year or so ago.' He coughed slightly and named a figure that for a dizzy moment made the whole office seem to revolve before Holly's eyes.

'But—but that's a fortune,' she whispered, thinking she must have misheard him.

'Exactly,' said Mr Windrush very dryly. He added, 'You must understand that this transfer will require a major reorganisation of the firm's financial assets, but we will proceed as quickly as possible. Those are Mr Kent's instructions.'

Holly stared at the solicitor dumbly. 'But—but that's impossible!' She was no financial expert, but she had been in the business world long enough to know that a company couldn't suddenly cut itself in half without risking bleeding to death. 'I mean—how could the company afford to do that and still carry on?'

The solicitor placed both hands on the desk in front of him. 'I can speak frankly to you, Mrs Ward. Indeed, I must, as you have asked that question. I believe that it would put a great—probably fatal—strain on the company's finances.'

'You mean—bankruptcy? The workers thrown out of a job?'

Mr Windrush shrugged significantly and didn't reply.

Holly sat silent, her head reeling as she tried to come to terms with what the solicitor had just told her. Mr Windrush watched her uneasily. The buzzer sounded on his desk and he said, 'Yes, ask her to wait, I shall only be a few minutes.' Then he coughed and looked at Holly. '—Er—Mr Kent asked me to draw up a short preliminary document for your signature, Mrs Ward.' He placed another sheet of paper before her.

Holly looked down at it and the black typewritten characters ran together. 'W-what is it?' she stammered.

'A formality,' the solicitor assured her with a keen look at her white face. 'Merely to acknowledge the position as far as it has gone. Actually it is hardly necessary at this point, but Mr Kent was anxious that you should confirm that you would abide by the decision of the two valuers who will be appointed— one by each of you.'

Holly's head was spinning. She pushed the paper away with shaking hands. 'I can't sign it. I couldn't accept all that money. Not from *him*,' she added violently.

Mr Windrush's bushy eyebrows seemed to quiver as they raised themselves. 'Mr Kent was quite definite. The legal position——' he began.

But Holly had got to her feet. 'I'm sorry, Mr Windrush.' She swallowed, putting a hand to her throat. 'This has been a shock. I—I can't take it in immediately. I'll have to have time——' Her throat dried up completely and she choked on the last words.

'Yes, yes, of course you will, Mrs Ward,' the solicitor said soothingly. He walked to the door and opened it quickly; he wouldn't want a hysterical woman on his hands. 'Now, you think it all over and then come back and talk to me again.' He held out his hand, and Holly took it briefly and stumbled down the spiral stairs and out into the sunlight.

The main street was busy after the lunch break. Holly walked along, her mind churning, narrowly missing collisions with women lugging shopping bags and visitors with cameras slung round their necks. She had to have a few minutes' quiet to adjust to the information she had just received. Her legs still felt weak and her mouth was dry.

She went into a shop that announced 'Teas' on a board outside. There was a counter piled with cakes on one side and a row of tables on the other. None of the tables was occupied and she sank into a chair at the first one she came to, which was the one in the window.

A woman in a flowery overall came from behind the counter. 'Nice after the rain,' she chatted affably. 'You visiting, dear? The season's getting over now, not quite so many folk about. Been rushed off our feet up to now, we have. What'll you have, dear? There's some nice scones, fresh from the oven.'

Tea was what Holly needed, but absently she ordered scones as well. When they came she poured out a cup of tea and gulped it down. She had to think what to do next, what to say to Jared Kent, and her brain didn't seem to be working properly. All she knew was that she had to tell Jared Kent in no uncertain terms that she didn't want his beastly money. She took a scone from the plate, cut it venomously in half and dabbed butter on it in blobs. That reminded her of the scene with Jared in the kitchen this morning. He really had behaved disgustingly to her.

She supposed, in a way, she knew why now. He must have been livid to find that under his father's will he had to share everything with Paul, whom he obviously despised and disliked. And even more livid when Paul's half of the business looked like passing to a girl he didn't even know.

Oh yes, she could see the reason for his hostility towards her, but that didn't excuse his beastliness. She bit into the scone, her even white teeth sinking into the crust as they had sunk into Jared Kent's flesh this morning. And she'd do it again if he tried to bully her, she assured herself. She couldn't wait to see his expression when she told him she wouldn't touch a penny of his money. When he knew he wasn't going to have to pay out he might even apologise for the way he had behaved to her. If he did she would laugh in his face.

Immersed in her dire thoughts of revenge, she looked idly out of the window at the passers-by. A man was approaching on the far side of the road, so tall that his dark head was inches above the heads of the other people near him. He came closer, and turned into Jared Kent. At the sudden unexpected sight of him her stomach clenched, and she sat like a statue as he stopped, thinking he might have seen her.

But no, he had met someone. A girl in a poppy-red dress with a cloud of silver-gilt hair swinging down her back came running up to him. Heads turned as they met; they made a spectacular pair, he so tall and dark, she petite and vivacious.

Holly watched them, fascinated. It was extraordinary to see Jared Kent smiling. He made some remark and the girl laughed up into his face and squeezed his arm, cuddling up against him.

It was like watching a film. The passers-by faded and only the two standing together across the road were in focus. Holly looked at the girl, pretty as any film star, laughing and flirting. And at the man, tall, and broad and dark, even from this distance exuding masculine sexuality as surely as any film idol. She saw the way his near-black hair curved behind his ears and shaped itself into his neck, the way his teeth glinted whitely in the deeply sun-tanned face when he smiled, and for a crazy moment she caught herself thinking: Perhaps when I tell him he'll smile at me like that. Perhaps when he knows I don't want to disrupt his life and upset all his plans he'll realise how wrong he was to hate me.

Perhaps——! She shook her head as if waking from a dream. What was she thinking of?

The two on the opposite pavement were parting now. The girl had her hand on Jared's arm and she stretched up on tiptoe and kissed him quickly, then ran off, a bobbing patch of scarlet among the crowd of pedestrians on the pavement. Jared Kent stood for a moment looking after her, still with that unfamiliar, whimsical smile softening his mouth. Then he raised a hand in salute and continued on his way.

A most peculiar pang shot through Holly. As if the man across the street were *her* man and not her bitter enemy. As if it were jealousy that was gripping her. She sat where she was and drank another cup of tea very slowly. The last thing she needed was to encounter Jared Kent face to face in the busy street. He wouldn't have any whimsical smile for *her*, that was for sure. A murderous glare, more likely.

When she thought he must be well out of the way she went to the counter to pay her bill. The woman in the overall pushed the change towards her. 'Everything all right, love?'

Holly stared blankly at her. 'What—oh yes, thank you, everything was fine.'

She noticed the trays of cakes on the counter. Oh goodness—Blanche's tea—she had promised. 'I'll take a dozen of those cakes, please. You choose for me. And could you tell me the nearest place to find a taxi?'

Holly hurried along the street, clutching the box of cakes, her eyes searching the doorways for the number of the taxi firm the woman had given her. She needed to get back to the house quickly, to be there, calm and composed, when Jared returned later.

Suddenly a hand shot out and grasped her arm, and she nearly dropped the box of cakes. She spun round and saw that she was passing the entrance to the solicitor's office and that she had walked straight into the path of the very man she had wanted to avoid, coming out of it.

She passed her tongue over her dry lips. 'I'm just going to find a taxi——' she began.

'No need,' he said curtly. 'I'm going home myself now, my car is round the corner. Come on.'

There was no help for it—she followed him to his car, parked in a side street, and got in when he opened the door for her. Within minutes they were out of the small town and heading up into the fells.

What wretched luck, Holly thought dismally. She'd had no time to plan in detail what she would say to him. Perhaps they could put off their confrontation until later. Trying a conversational tone, she said, 'I'm taking some cakes back for Blanche. She promised to get up and come downstairs for tea.'

'Oh yes? Well, she'll have to wait, I've got something to say to you first.'

He pulled the car into a gate-opening in the low,

slatey stone wall beside the road, slammed on the handbrake and switched off the engine. Then, in the sudden silence, he turned his gaze on Holly.

'I've seen Windrush again and he tells me you refused to sign the agreement he drew up.' He spoke tightly, as if he was controlling himself with an effort.

Holly raised her eyebrows. 'Yes, I did. I didn't think it was necessary.'

A flicker of pure rage passed over his face. 'I don't know what game you think you're playing, my girl, but whatever it is you're damned well going to come clean about it!'

'Don't speak to me in that tone! I won't be bullied.' She turned her head away and stared out of the car window, across the rolling fells with the high mountains rising beyond.

'Oh, for God's sake!' He wrenched the car door open. 'Let's get out of here and get some fresh air into all this.'

He came round and flung open the door on her side. Holly sat motionless, looking straight ahead, the box of cakes on her lap.

'Will you come out, or do I have to drag you out?'

Carefully she placed the cardboard box on the empty driving seat beside her and levered herself out of the car, avoiding any contact with the man who stood outside, grim as a jailer waiting for his prisoner to make a dash for freedom.

Jared opened the gate to allow them to pass through and as he was carefully closing it again she began to walk away over the damp grass, her one need to get as far as possible from him. Her breathing quickened as she climbed a steep rise in the ground, but she kept her mouth stubbornly closed. He climbed effortlessly beside her. At the top of the rise he gripped her arm, stopping her. 'That's far enough. I didn't come out for an afternoon stroll.'

There was a large flat rock beside her and he pushed her unceremoniously down on to it and stood towering over her.

'Now,' he said, 'talk.'

Holly stared up at him in silence, her mouth mutinous. Standing above her, his broad figure outlined against the blue of the sky, the wind ruffling his dark rough hair, his khaki shirt open at the neck, he looked magnificent, tough, frighteningly masculine. Hate him she might, but she had to admit that.

'Come on,' he said impatiently. 'Why did you refuse to sign that document? I don't know what game you're playing, but it won't work. You won't get a penny more out of me by using delaying tactics—and you know what will happen if you try, don't you? If you contest the valuation you'll simply be putting more money into the solicitors' pockets. They can make something like this drag on for years.'

Her eyes were on a level with the leather belt round his waist. She swallowed quickly and said, 'I'm not playing any game. I don't want your money—I told Mr Windrush so.'

He laughed contemptuously, and up here in the hills it was a harsh, primitive sound as it was borne away by the wind. 'Yes,' he said nastily. 'And he believed you as much as I do. Which is not at all. What woman would turn down what will amount to a small fortune?'

'You're looking at one now,' Holly said calmly.

He digested that for a moment and then lowered himself to the rock beside her. His face was only inches away as he said menacingly, 'So that's it, is it?

Do you think I'm stupid? What's the catch? Do you imagine I'll support you in luxury for the rest of your life?' His voice rose as he shot the questions at her, beating against her ears until she felt like screaming. 'Oh, I see your game now. You'll keep coming back for more and more—just as that husband of yours did. Squeeze, squeeze, squeeze, until I never know when the next demand will come or how much it will be. What a partner he turned out to be!'

He got restlessly to his feet again, glaring down at her. 'No, by God, I'm not going back to that!' He was shouting now. 'I'll pay out every penny it takes to get the whole rotten lot of you out of my life for good— and I'll make it stick!'

Holly stood up too, very straight, confronting him, her eyes blazing. 'You've had your say, now I'll have mine. I'd no idea when I came here that I would inherit anything at all. When you told me I was to have Paul's share I imagined it would be some fairly small amount—a few hundreds—a thousand pounds perhaps. But now I know what it is, I couldn't possibly take it. Paul never did anything to earn it, I know that only too well now, and just by being his wife for a few months I certainly haven't earned it either. And I won't take it from you, Mr Jared Kent.' Her voice rose and began to shake a little. 'You obviously feel you've been treated unfairly, but that doesn't excuse the way you've behaved to me since I came. I don't like you and I won't be in your debt. I'd feel——' she drew in a quivering breath '—I'd feel unclean.'

He looked down into her face, his eyes narrowed, his mouth curling. 'A very pretty speech, Mrs Ward,' he bit out. 'It's a pity it's all lies.'

Holly's eyes dilated, a red mist seemed to rise between their two faces. It was as if all her inside had turned molten; never in her life had she felt such fury. 'Oh, you—you bastard——' she gasped, raising her hand.

She saw his hand go up, but the adrenalin pouring into her bloodstream gave her strength and speed and she was too quick for him. She landed a stinging slap across his contemptuous mouth, and with a sob she turned and ran from him, her feet stumbling over the grass, the rough bracken tearing her legs through the thin nylon of her tights.

Through the pounding in her ears she could hear him running behind her and she increased her pace, up the next rise and then quickly down into a small dip. At this point he caught up with her, she could hear his breathing above her own raw gasps, could feel his hands on her.

She made a desperate effort to pull away, but the descent was too steep. She lost her balance and went rolling over and over down the hill, dragging him with her. They ended up at the bottom and Holly found herself flat on her back with the weight of Jared's body on her.

She was completely winded and she lay looking up into his face, her eyes wide and alarmed as she fought for breath. He levered himself on to his elbows, taking most of his weight off her, but still his body pinned her down beneath him. 'Well, well, well,' he said softly between his teeth, and his face was so close she could see the shining tips of his dark lashes as they swept his cheeks. 'So this is what it's all about, is it? You know what happens when you make a man angry, don't you, my pretty? You know all the tricks. Well, it would be a pity to disappoint you, especially after such a build-up.'

Holly saw his mouth lowering itself towards her. 'No,' she groaned. 'Oh no, you're wrong. I didn't——' She struggled helplessly, pushing against his chest with all her strength, not gaining an inch.

With a terrible fascination she saw his face come nearer and nearer. She fixed her eyes on his mouth. He was going to kiss her and there was nothing she could do to stop it happening.

Nothing, nothing, she thought desperately. And then it was as if her whole body was slowly melting, burning up.

Oh God, thought Holly, what's happened to me? I don't want to stop it. I *want* him to kiss me.

CHAPTER FOUR

His mouth closed over hers, and at the touch of his lips her whole body went limp. She had never known this before—this sharp, erotic stabbing of desire that ran through her blood. It was like putting a lighted match to a fuse and feeling the flame travel the length of it. His mouth explored hers and she felt him start to tremble against her as his kisses became deeper, demanding a response from her, forcing her lips to part. Almost deliriously she gave back kiss for kiss, suddenly not caring about pride, about self-respect, about dignity. She strained against him hungrily, her arms round his back, her body moving against his, revelling in the sensations that were giving her such exquisite pleasure, shudderingly sweet—different, far different, from anything she had ever felt before.

Then, suddenly, it had all changed. It was as if something snapped in him and he was out of control, a wild animal, biting, tearing her clothes off, his breath coming harshly as his mouth savaged her soft flesh. His hands were all over her—rough, hurtful, probing.

She was terrified now. 'No—no—please——' she panted, pushing at him with all her strength as he forced her down under him, his weight bruising her hips, her breast. Then she felt him lift away slightly, one hand fumbling with his belt, and she brought up her knee and pushed it into his stomach as hard as she could. He gasped and his hold on her slackened as the breath left his body. Holly rolled away and lay shuddering, her face against the damp, cold grass.

A huge sob rose inside her, and another, and another, and then she was weeping uncontrollably, her body shaking, the tears rolling down her cheeks as she gulped and hiccuped. It was as if all the misery of the last months was being released and pouring out on great waves of tears.

All sense of time had gone, but at last Jared's voice came from somewhere above her head. 'Stop it, Holly. For God's sake stop it!' A folded handkerchief was thrust under her cheek and she took it and pressed her face into it.

She felt his hands on her and she stiffened against them, but he said quite gently, 'It's all right now,' and somehow she knew it was, and let him lift her until she was sitting beside him on the grass, weak and limp. Her throat was aching, her eyes were blurred with tears and she was shivering with cold and tension.

'I'm sorry, Holly,' he said. 'I'm sorry.' And for a moment he sat with his head buried in his hands.

She wiped her eyes and blew her nose. 'I'd like to go back to the house,' she whispered, and he said, 'Yes, of course,' and helped her to the car, because her legs kept giving way under her.

They didn't speak again on the short drive. When the car stopped in front of the house Holly reached immediately for the door handle, but he put out a hand and stopped her. He said quietly, 'Come on, girl, don't hold it against me, I've said I'm sorry. What more can I say?'

She kept her head turned away. 'Nothing,' she muttered. 'I don't want you to say anything. I don't want to talk to you.'

'All the same, we have to talk,' he said. 'We're in this together, whether we like it or not. It seems that my father unwittingly bound us together and tied the knot very tight. We have to think of some way of untying it. Up to now we've both been overreacting, and I admit most of it's been my fault. I think we'd better draw a line and start again. Look, I'll buy you dinner night and we can discuss things in a civilised fashion, O.K.?'

Holly said quickly, 'I can't. There's Blanche, she'll need dinner——'

'Damn Blanche,' he said impatiently. 'Boil her an egg or something.'

He let go of her hand and she got out of the car. 'Oh, look!' she wailed. 'The cakes——!' The cardboard cakebox was wedged down between the gear lever and the corner of the front seat. 'They're cream cakes, they'll be squashed!'

Jared actually laughed. 'All in a good cause,' he said, retrieving the box and handing it out to her. Before she could work out what he meant by that he said, 'I'll get back to the office now and get some work done. I'll come back for you around seven,' and he put the car into gear and drove off with a swirl of gravel.

Holly walked slowly round the house to the side door and up the back stairs to her bedroom. Here she stripped off the cream suit and saw a green grass stain oozing across the back of the skirt and the short jacket. She stuffed the suit into a drawer and slammed it to. The suit was the last reminder of her wedding, and it was Jared's fault that it was ruined. There must be something significant about that, only she couldn't think what it was.

She stood beside the window, still shivering

spasmodically from shock and exhaustion, staring out over the brownish-green rolling grass of the fells. She had come near to being raped out there only a few minutes ago. Shame and humiliation tore through her as she admitted that she had asked for it, had let herself respond to Jared's kisses with an abandonment that shocked her rigid now that she relived those moments when she had clung to him, responding feverishly to his kisses. She must have been mad—but at that moment she had wanted him with a hunger that had something of madness in it.

She must be very, very careful not to get into such a situation again. And she must get away very soon. All that talk of his about them being tied together with a knot that they couldn't easily untie had to be—just talk. If a knot couldn't be untied it could be cut, and that was what she intended to do, she told herself firmly. Cut herself loose from a situation that threatened danger at every turn. She had had enough of pain and regret in the last few months; enough of mistakes and suffering for them.

As she showered and renewed her make-up to disguise the puffiness round her eyes, and got into the cords and top she had worn this morning, she began to plan how she would tackle Jared this evening. She would be calm and reasonable and not risk angering him again. That had been her fatal mistake, allowing anger to flare between them. It took two to make a quarrel, as they said, and she wouldn't allow herself to be needled by him again. Or manipulated either, she assured herself, as she made her way to Blanche's room.

She found that lady up and dressed, sitting before her mirror. She looked round and smiled in welcome as Holly entered the room. 'You see—I'm getting up,' she said, pleased with herself. 'Do you like this?' She stood up and twirled round to show off the powder-blue dress she was wearing. It was of fine wool, intricately embroidered, and announcing 'model' in every stitch. She sighed and pulled a face. 'I *have* lost such a lot of weight. This was quite tight on me before—before——' Her lip trembled.

'It fits you beautifully now,' Holly said hastily. 'You look great. And the colour's just right with your pretty hair.'

Blanche ran her fingers despairingly through her limp gold curls. 'Oh dear, I should have had my hair done. I just haven't had the energy to go into the town—it's always so crowded with tourists.'

'The crowds seem to be thinning out now,' Holly told her briskly. 'But I'll do it for you tomorrow, if you like. I can make it look nice until you feel up to going into the town.'

Blanche was turning this way and that before the mirror, patting the curls into place. 'Thank you, Holly, you're such a dear girl and so good for me. I feel a different person since you came.'

'That's how it's meant to be,' said Holly cheerfully. It didn't take much to make Blanche happy—not much more than it took to make the little cat downstairs happy. She wished that applied to the other member of the family. But Jared was a very different proposition. Jared—why must her mind keep returning to him all the time?

'I'll go and make the tea now,' she said, 'and we'll have it together when you come down. I've brought some cakes back with me. Cream ones—naughty but nice.' She smiled and left Blanche carefully applying lipstick.

In the kitchen Paws appeared from under the table, yawning and stretching and rubbing himself hopefully against Holly's legs, purring like an electric motor. 'More food?' Holly enquired, and put some milk in a saucer. A steady lapping noise followed. Holly sighed. 'Little Miss Sunshine, that's me,' she said wryly. 'I just wish someone would begin to straighten out *my* life for me.'

Perhaps this evening would see a change for the better, she mused, as she put the kettle on to boil and arranged the least squashed of the cream cakes on a pretty china plate with a flowery pattern. Perhaps Jared would be more reasonable and they could work something out between them.

Perhaps she could make him believe that she wasn't playing any deep and devious game and that she really didn't want any money from his company. Perhaps they might even be friends.

The kettle boiled and she filled the teapot impatiently. There were too many perhapses. And why, for heaven's sake, should she want to be friends with a man like Jared Kent?

Jared had said, 'Be ready at seven,' but in the event he returned soon after six. The afternoon with Blanche had, Holly reckoned, been quite successful. Blanche had enjoyed the cream cakes and drunk several cups of Darjeeling tea and talked endlessly about Paul—his childhood, his schooldays, his difficulty in choosing a career. 'He was so sensitive, poor boy, anything harsh or tough wouldn't have done for him.' Holly learned that he went to Art School for several years and after that, she gathered, he had drifted from one thing to another.

'It was so difficult for him, having no father,' Blanche lamented. 'My first marriage was a ghastly mistake, you see, and I had terrible trouble with the money arrangements. I had a little money of my own, fortunately, and we were able to get by for a time, but the worry of it made me quite ill. At last my doctor suggested a cruise would do me good—and it was on the cruise that I met my dear Clement. He was there for his health, too, he'd had a slight heart attack.' The blue eyes swam in tears. 'It was love at sight for both of us.' She clasped her hands on her lap and in the glow from the fire she looked youthful and pretty in an appealing, helpless way.

'My, my, what a cosy little domestic scene!'

Jared's voice from the doorway made both women start and look round. At the unexpected sight of him Holly felt that uncomfortable stir at the pit of her stomach again. 'You're back early.' She heard herself making the obvious remark as he strolled over and stood beside her chair, looking down at the two of them sitting there before the fire, with the little cat, who had appeared unnoticed, curled up on the rug.

'Quite a change to see you up and about, Blanche,' he said politely. 'Are you feeling better?'

Blanche's delicate hands clenched and she looked up timidly at him. He *had* been bullying her, the brute, Holly was convinced. No wonder the poor woman was in such a state!

'Much better, thank you, Jared.' The golden head turned to Holly, as if for reassurance. 'This dear girl has been so sweet to me.'

Jared's grey eyes fixed themselves on Holly, the dark lashes nearly covering them. 'Yes, she is a sweet girl,' he said. 'Indeed she is.' The words, spoken in that deep voice, sounded exactly as if he meant them. What was he up to now, the wretch?

'We're very lucky to have Holly here,' he went on shamelessly, and touched her shoulder lightly. 'We must try to persuade her to prolong her stay.'

Holly reacted to this amazing pronouncement with a jump of sheer surprise and felt the warning pressure of his hand increase.

She wasn't going to let him get away with this. 'I don't think——' she began.

But he continued as if she hadn't spoken. 'So we must look after her, mustn't we? I'm going to take her out and give her a good meal—if that's all right with you, Blanche? You won't mind us leaving you alone for a short while?'

Blanche's face was a study. Her pretty lips had been compressed as Jared came into the room, her blue eyes wary, but now she was relaxed, fluttering like a seventeen-year-old. 'No, of course I won't mind. I shall be quite happy. I think I'll go back to bed now, dear,' she added to Holly. 'I've been up long enough for the first time. There's sure to be a programme on TV tonight that I can look at, and you'll come in and see me when you get home, won't you?'

Holly gave it up—temporarily. She was beginning to know what a fly feels like when the silken strands of the spider's web close round it. 'I'll leave you some sandwiches and a flask of coffee and you can have them when you feel like it.' She held out a hand. 'Come along, I'll see you upstairs safely.'

Jared was waiting for Holly at the foot of the stairs when she came down an hour later, and he was looking, she had to admit, disturbingly handsome in black trousers, lightweight jacket and a finely-pleated white silk shirt that emphasized the deep tan of his neck. His thick dark hair was damp from his shower and had been tamed to lie almost—but not quite—flat on his well-shaped head.

His eyes passed slowly over her with masculine admiration as she reached the bottom on the stairs. 'Pretty dress—you look charming, Holly.'

Holly glanced warily at him, suspecting irony, but there wasn't a hint of it in his voice or his expression. He might have been any attractive man taking a girl out on their first date and admiring her dress.

It *was* a pretty dress, although its association made it impossible for Holly to like it any longer. Made of silk jersey, coral-colour, with a low, slashed neckline and long full sleeves gathered into deep cuffs, it clung lovingly to her slender figure, emphasising the tender curves of her neck and breast. She had bought it in Mexico for what had turned out to be her very last dinner with David Behrens. A dress for a romantic evening, she had thought, but that evening with David which had started in a blissful haze had ended in stark misery.

She had never been able to wear the dress again, but tonight it had seemed fitting that she should wear it for her dinner with Jared, which wasn't likely to turn out any happier—less traumatic, of course, because she had been in love with David and hadn't guessed that he was ruthless and callous, whereas she wasn't in love with Jared and he had shown her from the first that he possessed exactly the same hateful qualities.

But he certainly wasn't parading those qualities now, as he linked his arm with hers in a friendly fashion and led her out to the waiting car. He couldn't have been more courteous and urbane as he handed her into the passenger seat and arranged the skirt of her dress around her, his eyes flicking an upward glance of mischief as his hand rested for a moment on her silken ankles.

Holly's heart skipped a beat. Surely he didn't intend to flirt with her, as a preliminary to softening her up so that she would agree tamely to whatever arrangements he had in mind? If he did he was going to get the surprise of his life! Her body might react instinctively as it had just done, but her mind was ice-cool and resolved not to be hoodwinked again by any man's studied charisma. Twice was quite enough!

It was a beautiful, warm evening, and as they drove along in the dusk Holly felt the magical attraction of the place. The afterglow of the sunset still lingered in the sky, touching the lake, glimpsed now and again between the trees, with a rosy shimmer. The outline of the hills brooded over everything, darkly mysterious, and the mist was rising in the valleys, throwing a gossamer veil over the fields. The smell of pines drifted in through the open car window. The perfect run-up to a romantic evening, Holly thought, stifling a giggle and wondering why Jared had brought her here. Surely it would have been more appropriate to have their meeting at home in the morning? Or even at his office. Ah well, at least she would have a good meal, which was something she didn't seem to have had for days.

'Nearly there.' Jared's deep voice broke into her musings and he placed a hand briefly on her knee. He really was behaving just as if this were an important first date; as if he were out to charm her with subtle promises of shared pleasures to come.

Pooh! Holly thought as the car turned into a short drive and pulled up before the wide entrance of what had obviously once been a great mansion and was now a luxury hotel. He'll get nowhere like that. She wasn't Blanche, she assured herself, to flutter her eyelashes at him at the first sign (no doubt cynical) of flattering attention on his part.

So her small head, with its satin-smooth chignon of mink-brown hair, was held high as she walked beside him across the thick carpet of the entrance hall, where they were immediately approached by a dark-skinned waiter who beamed at Jared and announced that dinner would be served in ten minutes and would Mr Kent and Madam care to sit in the lounge where they could take aperitifs?

'I phoned the order through so that we shouldn't be kept waiting,' Jared explained, leading the way to a small table in a corner. 'I hope that's agreeable to you?'

Such politeness! 'Of course,' Holly murmured, and when her sherry was brought she sipped it in dignified silence.

Jared glanced round at the few other occupants of the lounge. 'Looks as if custom's thinning out,' he remarked conversationally. 'A week or two ago this place would have been bursting at the seams. But from September onwards and through October is when the real climbers and fell-walkers like to come, and then they count on—if not having the mountains to themselves—at least being able to get around in comfort.'

Holly was not to be outdone in small-talk. 'Do you climb yourself?' she enquired in a polite, conversational tone.

He shook his head. 'Not these days. Too busy. I sometimes scramble up Pike o' Blisco on a Sunday morning. It's fairly easy going and a grand view from the top on a clear day. I'll take you up there some time,' he added casually.

Holly blinked. What had he been going to say—and what was he getting at—talking as if she were a visitor on a long stay? He must know she had no intention of prolonging her time here, she'd made it plain enough. But before she could demur, the waiter arrived to usher them into the dining room, to a table for two beside a wide window, where the dark waters of the lake below were still visible in the fading light.

Holly left it to Jared to order wine, and looked around her. This was certainly a very smart restaurant—very expensive too, no doubt, with its crystal chandeliers, posies of flowers on the tables, glass and cutlery sparkling against white damask. Jared was certainly doing her proud, she thought, amused.

She watched him, dark and assured, as he conferred with the wine waiter, and again she felt that uncomfortable stirring at the pit of her stomach. He really was a very disturbing male brute—and 'brute' was the operative word. She turned away quickly and looked out of the wide, uncurtained window. It was almost dark outside now; she could just make out a paved terrace and a lawn sloping down to the shores of the lake, a streak of silver where the lights from the windows caught the edge of the water, receding into eerie blackness beyond. The focus of her eyes changed and the window itself became a black mirror, in which she saw Jared, looking up at the waiter as they talked, referring to the wine list, nodding thoughtfully.

Heavens, she thought irritably, can't I get the man out of my sights for a moment?

The waiter glided away and Jared turned to Holly with his dark-lashed smile. 'Now, I expect you to eat a large, nourishing meal. We must feed you up. I hazard a guess that you haven't been eating properly for some time—you're just a little too——' his eyes roamed over the bodice of her dress, lingering on the deep slashed neckline '—too slender. Only a very little, though.'

'Don't you mean skinny?' Holly said truculently. 'You prefer your girls on the plump side, do you?' She was thinking of the cuddly blonde who had kissed him in the High Street earlier, and her cheeks flamed as the words came out. What a stupid, provocative thing to say! He would think she was expecting to flirt with him over dinner, instead of having a serious talk.

He leaned back in his chair. 'I said slender and I meant slender,' he said quietly. 'I like a girl who fits my hand.'

Holly quivered inside as her eyes met his and it was as if he had touched her breast. She turned quickly to look out of the window again. 'Which lake is this?' she asked. 'I really haven't found out yet exactly where we are.'

She heard his deep chuckle and knew that his thoughts were following hers, but all he said was, 'Grasmere. One of my favourites, although they're all wonderful in their different ways. I expect I'm prejudiced, though, having lived here all my life, except for school and university.'

The waiter appeared beside the table at that point and as the meal progressed it was evident that Jared had decided to prove himself the perfect host. Taking Holly's silences for granted, he began to talk of the beauties of his part of England, of the mountains and lakes, the becks and fells and tarns.

Holly had to admit that he knew his subject, and that he knew how to make it interesting. He talked well, recounting how the Lake District came into being millions of years ago, a huge dome thrust up out of some ancient tropical sea, and then cracked to form valleys, which deepened over thousands of centuries with the action of glaciers melting after the Ice Age, making the lakes and rivers.

As gingered melon sprinkled with mint was followed by a succulent mixed grill with tiny new potatoes and petits pois, Holly began to relax and was almost able to enjoy herself. Jared kept her glass filled with a rosé wine, which she suspected was more potent than it seemed. She watched his face as he talked. The straight mouth had taken a softer line, the grey eyes with their long, curving lashes were devastatingly attractive, now that they were no longer glaring angrily at her.

As the meal progressed everything began to take on a hazy, warm friendliness that was reassuring. She got the feeling that they were two people who had just met and were beginning to get to know each other, to like each other. She wanted it to go on like this—impersonal, casual talk, that didn't threaten or disturb her. When Jared stopped talking and looked thoughtfully at her across the table she said quickly, 'Tell me about the people who lived here—the first ones, I mean.'

'Oh, it was all very Stone Age,' he said. 'You can still find bits of their axes and spearheads. The archaeologists have even discovered "factories" high up on the screes. There's one below Pike o' Stickle where the stone tools were apparently roughed out before they were sent down to the coast to be polished. When you go up there you can imagine those small, dark hairy men hacking away at the stone all the hours of the day.'

Holly sipped her wine and chuckled. 'Sounds like the Seven Dwarfs,' she said. 'Whistle while you work!'

She put down her glass quickly. She had certainly had too much wine and now she was making a fool of herself. But Jared wasn't looking superior; he was even laughing with her.

'That was a lovely meal,' she sighed, chasing the last crumbs of Black Forest gateau round her plate. 'I didn't realise I was so hungry.'

'Not quite over yet,' said Jared, and to the hovering waiter, 'Yes, thank you, we'll have coffee in the lounge.'

Facing her reflection in the mirror of the ladies' powder room a few minutes later, Holly wondered how she could have forgotten what they were here for. Jared had put himself out to entertain her, but that was a long way from a meeting of minds, she reminded herself. She had allowed the charming front he had chosen to put on to get inside her defences, but she must be on her guard again from now on. She wasn't going to allow him to have his own way about any arrangements they might make.

When she rejoined him in the lounge he patted a place beside him on a cushioned settee, but she pretended not to notice and took one of the tubby armchairs opposite instead. She saw the faint rise of his eyebrows but ignored that too and said brightly, looking round the room, where by now a few visitors were drifting in, 'This is a lovely place. Was it once a manor house, I wonder?'

When he didn't reply she looked up and saw that he was gesturing in greeting to someone across the room, a large, middle-aged man with white hair and a square amiable face. There was a girl with him who looked as if she had come straight out of a Hollywood soap-opera, cute and cuddly, with a mass of silver-gilt hair, her luscious figure spilling out of a jazzily-printed dress. It was the girl who had kissed Jared in the town this afternoon, and every man in the room was looking at her.

Jared sprang to his feet as they came across the lounge. 'Well, what d'you know?' the big man boomed heartily. 'Dawn here was telling me she met up with you earlier in the town, Mr Kent.' He pumped Jared's hand up and down.

The girl quirked her mouth at Jared. 'You didn't say you were coming to our hotel tonight.' She threw a glance towards Holly, who remained glued to her seat.

Jared followed the glance. 'Holly, this is Sam Robinson who's been good enough to do business with us in the past, and his daughter, Dawn,' he said formally, and to the two newcomers, 'My sister-in-law, Holly Ward. We've finished dinner—we were just about to have coffee. Won't you join us?'

Dawn gave Holly an all-over glance which Holly was sure took in every detail, chirruped 'Hi!' and immediately snuggled down beside Jared on the settee, while Holly found her hand enclosed in a huge paw and squeezed sympathetically as the white-haired man lowered himself into a chair beside her. 'Very glad to know you, ma'am. Mr Kent told me you were visiting. I'm sure sorry to hear about your loss.'

'Thank you,' Holly said, but she didn't seem able to take her eyes from the two on the opposite side of the table. Dawn was chatting away non-stop, gazing up into Jared's face with limpid blue eyes. He was smiling down at her lazily under his dark lashes.

Sam Robinson was, like his daughter, a talker. He declined an offer of coffee as they were going in to dinner forthwith. 'I've got a splendid appetite for it too,' he said heartily. 'There's nothing like walking on your—fells, do you call 'em?—to work up an appetite. I like to think of my forebears climbing up there the same way, many, many years ago.' He gave a great bellow of laughter. 'Dawn thinks I'm nuts to come to England searching for my roots, but she's a good girl, she comes along with her old poppa so he won't be lonely.' He lowered his voice, confiding, 'I lost my dear wife last year, it was a great blow.'

Holly murmured something sympathetic and he gave her hand a squeeze. 'But I still have my girl, thanks be. Pretty as a picture, isn't she?' He cast a loving glance at his daughter, who was devoting all her attention to Jared, giggling delightedly at something he said, resting her white hand intimately on his arm. 'I'm glad for her to have some young company. It's dull for her while I'm poking about among old church records.'

'Poppa,' his daughter squealed, 'Jared is going to show us his mill tomorrow, where they make all that lovely silk and stuff. Won't that be just great?'

'I'd be delighted if you'd both come,' Jared confirmed, and Sam Robinson nodded his white head and said they would make it a date.

Father and daughter were called in to dinner then and Jared turned back to Holly. 'Nice people,' he mused. 'Sam Robinson is a business contact, but he's come over here this time on an ancestor-hunt. His family left this district back in the eighteenth century and he's crazy to find out about them.'

More diners were drifting into the lounge now, and before Holly had had time to drink her coffee Jared had recognised several of them, and two separate middle-aged couples had come over to their table and been introduced to Holly and stayed chatting for a time, obviously interested in Holly and what she was doing there.

Jared was noncommittal, and when the second couple had departed he pulled a wry face. 'It's obvious we're not going to have our undisturbed talk,' he said. 'I suggest we go back home.'

He was silent on the drive back, and Holly puzzled over why he had taken her out to dinner at all, as he must have known they wouldn't be likely to be left alone. She came to the conclusion that Dawn Robinson was the attraction. He must have known that they would almost certainly encounter her and her father.

'Lucky meeting the Robinsons,' he said casually as they went into the house. 'Sam Robinson owns a chain of stores in Texas and they've given us several orders for our printed silk head-scarves.' He moved around, switching on lights. 'Brrh! it's chilly in here, I must get the central heating going. Let's go into my study, it'll be cosy there.'

Cosy—what an odd word to use in the circumstances! Up to now their relationship had been anything but cosy, Holly thought as she followed him into a small room leading off the hall which was almost filled by a big leather-topped table, piled with account books and papers and files.

'I do quite a bit of work here.' Jared leaned down to switch on the electric fire and immediately the sombre little room was filled with a warm glow. 'Wonderful invention, electricity,' he remarked chattily.

It was extraordinary, Holly thought, the change in the man. From the start of the evening his black mood had entirely disappeared and now he seemed extraordinarily pleased with himself and life. But of course! He had been planning to meet the Robinsons and issue his invitation, that would explain it. Poppa's little girl would be guaranteed to melt the hardest masculine heart. And good luck to her, Holly thought; she was welcome to him—*and* his moods.

There was only one seat in the room, a small leather sofa with just room enough for two people. Jared drew it up to the fire and Holly sat down stiffly in one corner. This was when she had to be on her guard, she reminded herself. Her resolution not to accept any part of Paul's share of the business hadn't weakened, and no doubt Jared's suspicions of her motive hadn't suddenly disappeared. It looked like stalemate.

He opened the door of a corner cupboard to a disclose bottles and glasses. 'I keep a small store here for when I work late,' he grinned. 'What'll you have? I'm afraid there's only whisky and beer.'

'Nothing, thanks,' said Holly.

'Or would you like some more coffee—or tea?' he urged. 'Wouldn't take a jiffy.'

'No, thank you,' she said again, firmly. For goodness' sake let's get on with it and get it settled, she thought. This whole evening had been one anticlimax after another.

Jared poured himself a whisky and, despite her refusal, put a glass beside her on the hearth containing about a tablespoonful of the same golden liquid. 'Just in case you change your mind,' he smiled.

'I don't——' Holly began, but he held up a hand, saying, 'Don't try to make me believe you're a girl who never changes her mind.'

'I'm not trying to make you believe anything,' Holly said impatiently as he sat down next to her—too near for her peace of mind. She drew in an exasperated breath. 'Look,' she said, 'don't you think it's time to get this thing settled? I thought we were going to discuss the position over dinner.'

'No hurry, is there?' he said easily. He took a swig of his drink and put his glass down, leaning back in his corner.

'It occurs to me,' he said, 'that it's rather odd that I don't know anything about you, Holly. You're my sister-in-law—well, stepsister-in-law—and I don't know where your home is, who your parents are.'

She shrugged. 'Nothing much to tell. I never really knew my parents. I was brought up by my grandmother, she died three years ago.'

He said quietly, 'What happened?'

'To my parents? We were driving home from Cornwall, after a holiday in my grandmother's cottage, and there was a bad storm. A tree fell across the car.' She was silent for a moment. Then she added, 'I was asleep in the back and I wasn't even scratched.'

'How old were you?'

'Two—three—something like that. They told me about it a long time afterwards.'

'And you don't remember anything about it?'

'No, nothing. I suppose it must be there somewhere tucked away deep down. I used to have bad dreams when I was a little girl. But I had a very happy childhood,' she added firmly, because she didn't want to let this man think she was making a bid for sympathy. 'Gran was marvellous to me and I miss her still.'

'And when you met Paul, in Mexico, you were living—where?'

This was getting a little too personal. She said shortly, 'I shared a flat in London. I was in Mexico on business with—with the man I worked for.'

To her relief he didn't probe any further, and she said again, 'Look, let's try to come to some agreement over my—inheritance, shall we? I want to get back to London as soon as possible and we must discuss the best way of settling things.'

Very deliberately Jared drained his glass and leaned forward to put it down beside the fire. Then, straightening himself slowly, he smiled at her, the grey eyes glittering under their ridiculously long lashes. She could feel the impact of that smile all through her body, like a fire creeping along her veins.

'Maybe, after all, there isn't anything to discuss,' he said.

Holly felt suddenly cold. Did he mean that he had come round to her point of view and that she would be leaving tomorrow after all? She was quite horrified at the sharp stab of disappointment she felt. That was all rubbish about wanting to get back to London. She hadn't meant a word of it. 'W-what do you mean?' she stammered.

He reached for her hand and covered it with his. 'I mean,' he said softly, 'that I'm asking you to stay, Holly. In view of the way I've behaved you may find it difficult to believe, but the truth is that I find that I can't do without you.'

CHAPTER FIVE

His hand gripped hers so hard that it hurt. 'What do you say—will you stay, Holly?'

The room seemed to revolve slowly before Holly's bemused eyes. Jared didn't hate and resent her. He was asking her to stay. He liked her, he needed her, he didn't want to push her out of his life. They would be friends, colleagues, and perhaps—as his eyes looked into hers her head swam with wonder at the eagerness she saw there. 'Yes, of course I'll stay if you want me to,' she heard her own voice say.

She was sure he was going to kiss her. He was so close, her arm was pressing against the crisp stuff of his shirt and the clean masculine smell of him was in her nostrils. Hardly aware of what she was doing, she slid further down into the soft leather-cushioned sofa so that her knee touched his hard-muscled thigh. She wanted with a painful longing to feel his arms go round her.

But instead he lay back in his corner of the sofa with a long sigh of relief. 'Well, that's splendid, I was afraid you'd say no. I'm sorry I gave you such a rotten welcome, Holly, but I couldn't know the kind of girl you are. You've been a surprise to me, I must admit. It threw me this morning when you took charge of the kitchen so competently and ordered me out of it. And the way you've handled Blanche already is just astonishing.'

He picked up his glass again and added complacently, 'Oh, it'll work out splendidly, you'll see. You're just what I need—someone who can run my house really efficiently. A million thanks, Holly, you're an angel. Let's drink to our partnership.' He picked up her glass and thrust it into her hand.

While he had been speaking Holly had had the sensation of ice creeping into her limbs from her feet upwards. Fool—idiot—moron! Of course he isn't really interested in you. He just needs you to take over the 'little woman's' job, to look after all the domestic arrangements that he can't cope with himself.

The change in his attitude—all that charm and friendliness—was just his male chauvinist way of acquiring a willing domestic slave. He had spun a web and she had walked straight into it.

The ice began to melt and a slow fire of anger to take its place. That she could have let herself be fooled yet again! It was almost too humiliating to bear. But bear it she must if she wanted to keep a shred of pride and self-respect. If she let him get the merest whiff of what she had been expecting she would die of shame.

'Come on, Holly, let's drink to it,' he was saying.

'Drink to what?' She forced the words between stiff lips.

'To our partnership, of course.' He sounded extremely pleased with himself now. 'It's a solution to our problem and we can make a real go of it together. I see that now. I'll be able to devote all my energics to the mill and you can have a free hand with the house here. It's gone to seed a bit lately, but I'm sure you can bring it up to standard.'

'Can I?' Holly said woodenly. She took a sip of whisky and coughed.

'Of course you can.' Jared laughed and pressed her

hand. 'Oh, I'm not suggesting you toil over the kitchen sink or a hot stove. We'll find proper staff somehow. Then I'll be in a position to entertain—it's so necessary in business, as I expect you realise. I'd like to invite Sam Robinson and Dawn for a meal while they're in the district. But perhaps that would be expecting too much of you for a start?'

Holly took another sip of whisky and this time she didn't cough. 'Oh, I dare say it could be managed,' she said coolly. 'That is, if we can find some staff. Any suggestions?'

She felt quite pleased with her offhand manner. The whisky was helping, of course. The way she had rapped out that question they might have been at a board-room meeting. Partners, he had said. All right, that was how it would be. Business partners.

He was laughing at her. 'Holly! You sound as if——' He paused.

'Yes?' She raised her eyebrows.

He made an impatient gesture. 'Oh, never mind. Staff? Well, we used to have a couple—a man and wife called Burkett. They were very good. They worked here for us for years until my father died. Then Blanche took over and Paul began to throw his weight about and there was trouble, and eventually the Burketts packed it in. I believe they're now living with a married daughter in Ambleside. I daresay you could persuade them to come back—it's worth a try.'

Holly nodded, pulled a notepad across the desk and wrote down the address he gave her. 'I'll go and see them tomorrow. And that raises another point—what about transport for me?' She shot the question at him.

He blinked. 'Yes, of course, you'll need transport.

My father bought Blanche a car, but she hasn't driven it for months, to my knowledge. You drive?'

'Of course.'

'Of course,' he said rather drily. 'Well, I'll get it started up for you in the morning and it can be serviced as soon as the garage can do it.'

'Fine.' She drank some more whisky. Dutch courage, they called it, didn't they? She gritted her teeth. Carry on, Holly.

'And another thing—how do you suggest I draw my income? I take it that as we appear to be equal partners we shall draw equal incomes from the business and share the household expenses. Perhaps I could have access to the firm's books soon and then we can settle the details?'

Jared was looking at her very oddly. 'Er—yes, of course.' He got up and poured himself another drink.

Holly stood too, glancing at her watch. 'I'll go up now. I promised to look in and see Blanche as soon as we got back. And then I think I'll go straight off to bed, I feel a bit tired. Remnants of jet-lag, I expect.' She walked to the door. 'Breakfast will be at eight. Will that suit you?'

'Perfectly,' he said in a stunned kind of voice.

She smiled pleasantly at him. 'Thank you for the dinner, it was lovely. We can plan further tomorrow for our—partnership. Goodnight, Jared.'

She closed the door behind her and leaned against it for a moment, breathing rather quickly. Then she ran up the stairs as if pursued by furies.

Blanche's door was ajar and Holly peeped in. The TV was turned low, flickering and jabbering at the foot of the bed. The bedside lamp was still on; the plate that had contained the sandwiches now contained nothing more than a few crumbs and a curled-up piece of cling-film; the coffee flask was empty. And Blanche was fast asleep, her golden curls encased in a net, her cheeks shiny with skin cream. Blanche had begun to take an interest in her appearance again. Holly turned off the TV and the light and tiptoed out of the room.

Her own bedroom was cold. She pulled the curtains and stood holding on to them as she heard the stairs creak under heavy footsteps which stopped outside her door. Her teeth bit into her lip and she froze. After what seemed an age the stairs creaked again. A door closed below.

She sank on to the bed and began to laugh, and went on laughing until the laughter turned at last to tears and she buried her face in the pillow and wept with disappointment and humiliation.

Holly had less than two hours' sleep that night and was woken by the soft buzz of her travelling alarm clock. She groped for it, groaning, and switched it off. She had endured a wretched night, but somehow she had got her thoughts into order and made her plans before she finally fell asleep. And one thought emerged now, clear and definite—not if it killed her would she fail to have breakfast on the table at eight o'clock for *that man*.

Programmed by five years of disciplining herself to arrive at the office on time, she lurched out of bed and pulled back the curtains. It was raining again, a thick grey curtain that swept across the fields and shrouded the tops of the mountains. There was no sound but the bleating of sheep, a lost, melancholy chorus. She wondered what it would be like when winter really set in. Cold and bleak and depressing, no doubt, but it had to be endured. She had been tricked into taking this job on, but she would see it through, one day at a time. Keeping this thought firmly in mind, she started to dress in businesslike jeans and a belligerently scarlet top.

Jared came out of his study as Holly reached the bottom of the stairs. In dark trousers and a cream roll-neck sweater he looked alert and freshly-groomed, and in spite of her overnight resolutions her heart gave a heavy thump at the sight of him.

But her voice was steady as she said, 'Good morning. You're up already—would you have preferred breakfast earlier? Half-past seven?'

'Good morning, Holly.' He smiled at her cheerfully. 'No, eight will do splendidly. I usually like to put in some paper-work before breakfast. I made coffee, by the way, and I've let the cat out.'

'Thank you.' Holly registered a vow to be up earlier tomorrow.

She went into the kitchen and he followed and sat himself down at the table, watching her while she got out plates and cutlery and put bread in the toaster.

'There doesn't seem to be any bacon,' she said. 'Would you like an egg?'

'An egg would be splendid. Scrambled, if that's not too much trouble.'

'Of course not,' she said politely. She wished he would go away, not sit there following her every movement with those gunmetal grey eyes of his that seem to see right through her. But finally the eggs were cooked and she put the plate on the table before him.

'Looks good.' Jared eyed the creamy yellow heap on its double slice of toast with satisfaction. 'Aren't you having any?'—as Holly sat down opposite.

'I don't usually have a cooked breakfast,' she said, helping herself to a slice of toast.

'Oh dear!' He registered mock-dismay. 'You haven't done this specially for me?'

She scraped butter on the toast. 'Wasn't that the idea? You said you needed domestic help. I'm quite prepared to earn my keep by providing that—until I find someone capable of taking it on,' she added pointedly.

'And then?'

She had thought this out during the wakeful hours of the night. 'Then I suggest that I begin to take my place in the business.'

She had the satisfaction of seeing a look of horror cross his face.

'Take your place? What do you know about a textile mill?'

'Nothing, but I can learn.' She munched the toast, but had to take a mouthful of coffee before she could manage to swallow it.

He was looking decidedly uneasy and annoyed now. 'That's rubbish. There's absolutely no need for you to concern yourself with the running of the firm. All right, so we're partners, that's been wished on both of us and I accept your half-interest. But I'm in charge of things and I warn you I don't intend to——'

'To have an ignorant woman interfering?' Holly put in.

'Quite,' he said crisply.

'Don't worry, Jared, I shan't make a nuisance of myself. But I can't accept my share of the profits without doing something to earn it. Partners, you said so yourself.'

'I'm not worried,' he barked. 'And I'm damned sure

you're not going to make a nuisance of yourself—I'll
see to that!'

They glared at each other across the t^ ^ . And
suddenly, it was as if the grey eyes cl^ ^ ^ with the
brown ones set up a sizzle of electricity between them.
Holly felt it running through her, charging up her
whole body with a quivering energy. She looked away.
This was absurd, she couldn't go on letting him affect
her like this. She passed her tongue over dry lips.
'You're being very——' she began.

And stopped, because there was something about
the silence on the other side of the table that got to
her, even though she wasn't looking that way.

She dragged her eyes back to him reluctantly and
saw that he was smiling, a thin, devilish smile. 'We're
quarrelling again, Holly,' he said. 'And you know
what happened last time you provoked me.' He got up
and came round and stood behind her, putting both
hands on her shoulders, his fingers digging into her
soft flesh. 'Is this by way of being an invitation?'

At his touch a thrill ran through her whole body.
'No,' she gasped quickly, wriggling from his grasp.
'Don't be silly, Jared, I wasn't trying to provoke you.
I just wanted to make it clear that I intended to earn
my income. And anyway, the matter doesn't arise yet.
It will take me a little while to get the house organised
and cleaned up. I'm afraid your daily women haven't
been very thorough.'

He went back to his chair again with a grimace and
drained his coffee mug. 'Quarrel over. A pity, I was
just beginning to enjoy it. But no doubt we shall
repeat the performance, and that will be something to
look forward to.'

Before she could think of a retort his expression had

changed and when he spoke again it was the
businessman speaking, the man whose attention had
left the breakfast table and petty domestic details, and
was already fixed upon the day's important work
ahead.

'I've got Blanche's car started for you,' he said
briskly. 'It's outside at the front. The engine's a bit
sluggish, you'd better get her serviced. If you're going
to look up the Burketts you could call in at the
garage—it's Fox's in Ambleside—and make an
appointment. Or they might do it while you wait.'

He took a wallet from his pocket, extracted a cheque
and tossed it over the table to her. 'And you can call in
at the bank at the same time and draw out some cash.
I'll ring the manager from the mill when I get there
and tell him you're coming, and make an appointment
for us both to go in and see him. We'll have to re-
vamp the various accounts, but we can talk about that
later. Make the best arrangements you can with the
Burketts. If they're prepared to come back they'll no
doubt want us to up their wages. If not, you can see
about advertising for someone.'

'Yes—sir,' said Holly. 'Any more instructions?'

Jared was on his feet now and he looked down at her
and laughed, white teeth flashing in his brown face.
'Sarcasm, eh? Watch it, my girl, you're tempting fate!'
He picked up his briefcase from the chair beside him
and strode to the door. 'See you,' he said without
looking back—and was gone.

Holly sat there feeling as if she'd been out in a storm
in a small boat. Damn the man, he was clever, he knew
how to get under her skin. But she would hold her
own if it killed her, she would just have to be very
careful not to give him an excuse to lose his temper. If

he wanted dalliance he could get it from Dawn Robinson, who wouldn't be at all averse, as she had plainly shown yesterday in the hotel.

That reminded her that Jared was showing the Robinsons over the mill this afternoon. Big deal—she hoped they all had a marvellous time.

Suddenly charged with nervous energy, she jumped up and clattered the breakfast dishes together, preparatory to washing them up and tidying the kitchen before it was time to take Blanche's breakfast up. But she certainly wasn't going to be the domestic help for long, she assured herself, as she tried to squeeze the last drop of washing-up liquid out of an empty container. She hadn't spent a year at secretarial school and another year attending evening classes in order to learn how to scrub and polish. She didn't object to housework—quite enjoyed it, in fact—so long as there were other, more interesting demands on her as well.

What do you know about a mill? that man had asked her contemptuously. Well, the answer had been nothing, of course. But when the product was made, it had to be sold, and that, Holly promised herself, was where she would come in.

As she went about the house jobs she began to plan. She would phone Luis Ferida in Mexico City—she wanted to speak to him anyway, to let him and Juanita know that she had arrived safely and to thank them again for their kindness and help. And she could mention the contacts she had been making out there on Paul's behalf, and suggest there might be more openings for the marketing of Kent and Son's products. It would be a way of pulling her weight in the firm, and Jared would see how capable she was and what an asset she could be, and he would drop the 'little woman' act and be *glad* to have her for a partner.

After that Holly's day proceeded more smoothly. Blanche was a different woman this morning from the limp, half-drugged wreck she had been yesterday. She smiled brightly when Holly took up her breakfast tray and clapped her hands like a child as she looked at it— 'You're spoiling me, Holly. How lovely!' and said that she would get up for lunch today.

As Holly reached the kitchen again the little black and white cat leapt in through the open window and proceeded to weave himself round her legs, purring ecstatically. She leaned down and stroked his velvety neck. 'Only bread and milk again, I'm afraid, Paws,' Holly told him. 'But I'll buy you some real food when I go out. How would you feel about sardines?'

She looked into the fridge, clicked her tongue and sat down to make a list.

Blanche's red Mini was standing at the front door and started without much urging. There was an A.A. book on the parcel shelf and Holly studied it, finding the roads to Windermere, to Ambleside, getting an idea of the general layout of the country around. She had never owned a car, but she had taken her test as soon as she landed her first job with David Behrens's firm, and when she became his secretary she had driven his big flashy car frequently, so the Mini presented no problems.

By the time she reached Ambleside and found a place to park the rain had stopped and weak sunshine was breaking through, turning the grey, slatey roofs of the buildings to silver and giving a freshly-washed look to the little town. The roads were winding, untidy straggles of shops converted from houses, interspersed with some houses still remaining, and Holly wandered around, getting her bearings, looking in at shop windows. There was one stacked with climbing gear and equipment. She didn't think she would be much good at real climbing, but she certainly intended to do some fell-walking when the time presented itself. In any case, she thought, pausing before a window that displayed beautiful hand-knitted jumpers and chunky jackets, she would need a complete new outfit of clothes if she were to spend the winter here in Cumbria.

Suddenly the prospect began to feel bearable— exciting almost. This was a part of the world she could grow to love, with its spectacular grandeur of scenery, its mountains and lakes, its fells and trees and sweeps of grassland, its low whitewashed houses and its myriad sheep. The well-known beauty spots would be crowded in the summer—she had heard about that already. But there would be hard weather and a primitive remoteness about the place out of the season—a wildness that called to her in her present mood.

For the first time she felt a certain pleasure in the way things were going, instead of incredulity and anger and resentment and—yes, face it—guilt too. Because there was still this feeling that she didn't deserve to accept Paul's inheritance. She hadn't ever really been a wife to him. She wondered if she could, later on, explain everything to Jared and if he would listen to her and understand.

That had been a crazy moment, last night, when she had imagined he wanted her to stay because he had fallen in love with her. Equally crazy to think that she had fallen for him. And she had been silly and immature to take umbrage because he had said he needed her to look after the domestic arrangements. Surely, now, they could begin again on a more friendly basis—become partners, as he had suggested?

She would have to be careful to avoid getting herself into any situation that spelt danger, because she admitted that he had a strong physical attraction for her—he was a very sexy man, as she had recognised right from the first moment she saw him. And he had shown her that—manlike—he would amuse himself with her if she gave him the opportunity. Yes, she must be careful. She stood for a moment in the busy street as people passed by: warmly-clad women with baskets and prams and toddlers; tourists with cameras slung round their necks; businesslike climbers in hefty boots and waterproofs, with packs hitched on their backs. Then she shook her head free of the memory that was disturbing her and pulled out her shopping list.

By the time she got back to the house the strangeness of her position had begun to mellow and the low white house, set against its background of dark trees, looked almost like home. Blanche was downstairs, trailing round vaguely and ineffectually in the kitchen, clad in a jade-green silk wrapper, her golden hair piled high on her head and her pretty face carefully made up. She had spread a red and white checked cloth on the table and that was as far as she had got with preparing lunch, but at least she had risen from her bed, and that was a start.

She sank down into a cushioned basket-chair with an exhausted sigh as Holly came in, but her face brightened when the shopping bags were unpacked, and when a ham and mushroom quiche appeared she beamed with delight.

Holly had managed to get the Aga going before she left this morning, and the big kitchen was pleasantly warm. 'This *is* cosy,' sighed Blanche as they sat down at the table. Then she frowned. 'I do hope Jared isn't coming home for lunch.'

Holly shook her head. 'He's lunching with some people called Robinson—we met them last night—and showing them over the mill this afternoon.' She had a sudden picture of Dawn ooh-ing and aah-ing and clinging to Jared's arm, and began quickly to talk about her morning's shopping activities. 'And I've seen that couple who used to work here—the Burketts—and arranged with them to come back for a month's trial to see how we all get on. They're living with their married daughter and I got the feeling that it wasn't working out too well.' That was a tactful fabrication, but it wouldn't be wise to let Blanche guess what Mrs Burkett had said about her reasons for leaving in the first place. Actually it hadn't been too easy to persuade Mrs Burkett, who was a small, wiry woman with deep-set darting black eyes that proclaimed she was nobody's fool. She had been very stiff with Holly at first, but after explanations she had unbent slightly.

'We worked for old Mr Kent and Mr Jared for ten years, me and Joe, and never a cross word,' she said, sitting upright on the edge of her chair and folding her hands on her apron. 'But it all changed when Mr Kent married again. His wife wanted waiting on hand and foot—got me cooking special little dainties for her and washing her underclothes every day. And that son of hers, Paul, a proper layabout he was.' She grimaced, and then remembered who Holly was. 'I'm sorry, missus, as you're his widow an' all, you tell me, but I

couldn't forgive him for what he did to Mr Jared, and
him working so hard at t'mill to support the lot of 'em,
and looking forward to getting married, too. He's a
fine man, Mr Jared, and he deserved better.'

Looking forward to getting married! Holly was
completely out of her depth. She waited, hoping for
further elucidation, but beyond stating that, 'Joe and
me will come back up on Monday and see how we get
on then. I'll tell Joe when he gets in,' Mrs Burkett said
no more and rose from her chair.

Holly had felt herself dismissed. She was obviously
on probation and if Mrs Burkett didn't approve of her
she would pack their bags and be off again. She smiled
at the little woman, rather liking her independence,
said she would look forward to seeing them both, and
drove back to the house with her fingers crossed on
the car wheel.

Blanche, fork raised to her mouth, wrinkled her
nose now when Holly told her of the Burketts'
proposed return, remarking that they were a surly
couple but she supposed they were better than the
daily women who had been coming lately, and Holly
registered a silent vow to keep Blanche and Mrs
Burkett well apart.

'You must let me look after all the domestic
arrangements for a while, until you're quite better,'
she suggested tactfully. 'You won't feel hurt if I take
over the reins, will you?'

Blanche laughed her pretty laugh. 'My dear child!
I'll be only too pleased. Keeping house isn't really in
my line, you know. Coming to live here was a bit of a
shock, I can tell you, although dear Clement did his
very best to make me happy and comfortable. But the
Burketts were always rather a trial. Perhaps you'll be

better at dealing with them.' She lost interest in the subject and applied her attention to her quiche.

After lunch Blanche announced that she would go to her room and 'have a little rest'. 'I mustn't overdo things at first,' she said.

Holly almost laughed at the idea that Blanche had been overdoing things, but restrained herself in time, and in any case she would get on faster with the housework with Blanche out of the way. She was determined to have the whole place spick and span by the time Mrs Burkett returned on Monday.

She worked hard for a couple of hours, dusting, polishing, hoovering, and all the time Mrs Burkett's words kept nagging at her mind '—and Mr Jared looking forward to getting married.' Who and where was the unknown fiancée? Were they still engaged? If Jared announced one day that he was going to be married what would happen to their 'partnership' then? She carried her cleaning gear back to the kitchen, trying to put the question out of her mind, thinking that she would have time for a shower before making tea for Blanche.

She didn't hear the car pull up at the front, and when the kitchen door swung open and Jared appeared she gave a little gasp of surprise and put down the Hoover with a thud. The unexpected sight of him standing there, handsome and arrogant, filling the kitchen with his masculine presence, made her heart thump against her ribs.

He stood looking at her for a moment, under his long, dark lashes, and he seemed to be smiling. 'Hullo,' he said softly. 'Busy?'

Holly put a hand to her hair, damp from her exertions. 'I've just finished doing the drawing room,' she said. 'I was going to have a shower and tidy myself up. All this housework——' she muttered, suddenly self-conscious. 'I must look a mess.'

He sauntered across the kitchen and stood in front of her, and suddenly she found herself unable to move. 'You make a charming Cinderella,' he said softly. 'And you've got a smut on your cheek.'

He lifted his hand and slid a finger down her cheek, and Holly's inside melted at his touch. Damn the man, how dared he practise his sexy techniques on her? She stared up indignantly into his eyes, so close to her own. And then, inevitably, the current flowed between them, electric, vibrant, and his arms reached for her. There was a moment when he held her loosely, smiling into her eyes, when she could have pulled away if she had chosen, but her limbs were weak as water and when his mouth came slowly down on hers she groaned with the intense pleasure that spread through her body.

He kissed her slowly, sensuously, as if savouring some new, delightful experience, and she closed her eyes and responded intuitively, her lips parting sweetly to his, while the two of them clung together, swaying like dancers whose steps fitted perfectly.

When at last he drew away she felt like weeping and reached for the table to steady herself. He held her at arm's length, both hands on her shoulders and his eyes, searching hers, glinted under their long, dark lashes. 'Well, well,' he murmured, and then, smiling regretfully, 'This must rank as unfinished business, I fear. We have visitors. Dawn and her father are in the drawing room. I invited them back to tea—will you produce some for them, Holly?'

Humiliation burned inside her. If he had smacked

her face she couldn't have felt worse. It was an insult—the master amusing himself kissing the housemaid while visitors sat waiting in the drawing room!

'Oh,' she gasped, 'you expect a lot, don't you?' The ill-chosen words were out before she had time to consider their implication.

His smile broadened. 'Maybe I do, Holly,' his eyes and his voice leaving no doubt that he was deliberately misunderstanding. 'And not without encouragement, it seems,' he added very softly.

He turned and walked to the door. 'Don't be too long,' he said, and went back to his visitors.

CHAPTER SIX

HOLLY stood shaking, appalled that she could have been so weak. Jared had treated her as the master might have treated a housemaid in one of those old films. *Oh!* she muttered furiously, stam-ing her foot and slamming her hand on the table. I'd like to—to——

And what *would* you like, you idiot girl? She bit her lip. All right, face it, you'd like to be in his arms again. To put it crudely, what you feel for this man is merely lust, so snap out of it, can't you?

Thoroughly disconcerted, she switched the kettle on, set tea-things on the trolley, and buttered the scones she had brought in with her. While the kettle was boiling she swilled her face under the tap and tidied her hair, using the comb from the little vanity case in her handbag. The mirror told her that, devoid of make-up, and with her hair flattened down, she looked less than eye-catching. Well, that was O.K., she certainly wasn't in competition with Dawn Robinson. As she carried the tray into the drawing room she reflected somewhat sourly that she ought to have been wearing a frilly cap and apron to complete the picture.

Blanche must have come downstairs when she heard the car arriving and voices below. She was sitting next to Sam Robinson, their chairs pulled close together, deep in conversation. Her cheeks were pink, her eyes sparkling like sapphires, while the big American looked almost bemused as he bent towards her, listening. Dawn and Jared were also close together, on the sofa, her hand resting on his knee as she gazed up at him languishingly.

That was the picture that presented itself to Holly as she opened the door. Then both men got to their feet, Jared took the tray from her while Sam Robinson said in his booming voice. 'This is very civil of you, Mrs Ward. I hope we're not intruding, but Jared wanted us to see his home. You sure have a lovely place here, with that view and everything.' He waved his hand towards the window, but he was gazing at Blanche. She was looking dainty and charming in a soft wollen dress, a double string of pearls round her neck and her golden curls piled on top of her head. Sam Robinson couldn't take his eyes off her.

Jared, apparently, couldn't take his eyes off Dawn, as she cuddled up beside him on the sofa, her legs, encased in tight scarlet jeans, tucked under her, her fluffy white top brushing against his arm.

Holly poured out tea, feeling like a spare part to this cosy foursome, and wondered how soon she could escape.

Dawn was flattering Jared blatantly. 'I just *adored* your mill, Jared, I think you're wonderful, the way you run it all. And that *gorgeous* scarf you gave me—it just blew my mind. Wasn't it all great, Pop?'

He father dragged his eyes away from Blanche. 'I'll say it was. I know a well-managed business when I see one.' He beamed at Holly. 'I must congratulate yourself and Jared, ma'am. He tells me you and he are working partners.'

Holly saw Jared's mocking smile directed at her and looked away quickly as Dawn sighed and regarded her as if she were some sort of rare animal. 'I think it's just

fan*tas*tic how a *girl* can know about all those great
machines and things. I wish poor little me wasn't too
dumb to understand it.' She giggled and cuddled
closer to Jared, and he smiled down at her under his
dark lashes and squeezed her hand.

'You have lots of other accomplishments to make
up, my sweet,' he said softly.

Sam began to talk to the company in general, telling
them about his chain of stores in Texas. Blanche hung
on to his every word with parted lips while Jared put
in interested questions now and again, and Dawn
rested her head against his shoulder.

Holly sat beside the table and poured out tea and
felt as if her smile was painted on to her mouth. As
soon as everyone had had second cups and the plate of
scones was nearly empty she escaped to the kitchen
with a murmured excuse. The little cat was curled up
in the chair beside the Aga and Holly leant down and
rubbed her cheek against his soft fur. 'At least you
love me, don't you, Paws?' she said, and he mewed
feebly and settled back to sleep again.

Jared appeared a few minutes later, carrying the
tray. He put it on the table and said, 'We're all going
for a bit of a run around and then back to the hotel.
Sam wants to entertain us for dinner. You're invited
too, Holly. Want to come?'

'You needn't sound so enthusiastic,' Holly said
coldly. 'No, thanks, as a matter of fact, I don't. Four's
company, five's a crowd,' she added. 'And anyway, I
have to put a phone call through to Luis. All right if I
use the phone in your study? And do you happen to
know how many hours back Mexico City is?'

'Six,' he said. 'Or seven, I forget.' He frowned.
'Why do you have to ring Luis?' He wandered

across the kitchen and scratched the cat behind his ear.

'Why not? Luis was very kind to me. I liked him. And his sister too, I'm very fond of both of them.'

'Oh yes?' He sounded uninterested now. He had probably thought it was something to do with business. 'Well, I'll tell Sam you don't want to come, shall I?'

'You couldn't be a bit more tactful and say I have a headache, could you?' said Holly, beginning to pile the dishes into the sink.

'I could,' he turned to the door, 'but I'm not much good at social niceties.'

'You seemed to be doing all right with Dawn,' Holly snapped, and could have bitten her tongue out.

She had her back to him and couldn't see the way he grinned. 'See you later, then,' he said, and went out.

A few minutes later Holly heard the car drive away. When she was quite sure that they had all left the house she went into Jared's study and dialled the call to Mexico, to Luis's office.

Luis sounded absolutely delighted. 'My dear 'Olly, but this is splendid!' Luis spoke perfect English except that his h's were a bit shaky.

''Ow are you, and did you have a good flight? I 'ave been thinking so much about you, and wishing I could have come with you to look after you.'

Holly was touched. She had a picture of Luis in Mexico City, looking handsome and macho in his office suit, his black hair brushed back impeccably, his sloe-dark eyes admiring her openly, Spanish-fashion. 'How sweet of you, Luis, but I managed very well. I'm staying with Paul's family now, right up in Cumbria, in the Lake District.'

They chatted for a few minutes and Holly asked after Juanita, then Luis said, 'I am planning to visit your country next week.' He seemed to hesitate. 'I would so much like to see you, 'Olly, if that could be arranged.'

'Oh yes,' she said warmly. 'It would be lovely. Could you come up and stay with us here for a few days?'

'That would be a great pleasure,' Luis said eagerly. 'Mr Kent, would he be agreeable, do you think? I 'ave never 'ad the pleasure of meeting him, only by telephone and letter.'

'I'm sure he'd be delighted,' said Holly. It didn't really matter whether he would or not, *she* would be delighted, and that was the important thing. They talked for a few minutes more and Holly sent her love to Juanita, and Luis promised to phone the moment he arrived in England. As they said goodbye and Holly put the receiver back on its cradle she was smiling. It was wonderful to speak to someone who had proved to be a real friend.

She sat for a moment looking round the office where Jared worked. The huge desk with its tiers of brass-handled drawers might have belonged to his grand-father. On the top a stack of papers was anchored by a glass paperweight with a picture of Windermere inside it. Account books, reference books, jotting-pads lay about. It wasn't particularly tidy, but Holly guessed that Jared could put his finger on anything at a moment's notice.

She had wanted to look up the international code to Mexico and had eventually found the phone book in one of the desk drawers. Now, as she tried to put it back, it wouldn't fit in properly. As she pulled out the

other books in the drawer an unframed studio-
photograph fell out from between them on to the floor.
She stared down at it and a girl looked back at her, a
stunningly beautiful girl, with clouds of black hair and
huge violet eyes and a mouth that was frank invitation.
In the corner was scrawled, To my darling Jared. All
yours always, Vivienne.

Holly picked up the photograph and held it gingerly
between finger and thumb, as if it were dangerous. A
face like that might have appeared on the cover of any
glossy fashion magazine, but instead it was tucked
away in Jared's desk. His fiancée, certainly. Perhaps
his ex-fiancée, as it wasn't on show, framed, on the top
of the desk. But he had kept it. Whatever had
happened between them, he had kept her photograph.

Suddenly Holly didn't want to look at it any longer;
it was nothing to do with her. She pushed it back
where it had come from and hurried out of the study.

But all through the evening, while she watched TV
with Paws curled up on her knee, the face of the girl in
the photograph kept coming between her eyes and the
screen. She went to bed early and her bedside light
was switched off by the time she heard Jared and
Blanche come home. She turned over in bed and
pulled the duvet over her ears. She didn't want to hear
Jared's voice tonight.

The Burketts returned on Monday morning, delivered
at the back door by their son-in-law. Mrs Burkett
stood in the kitchen, her tweed coat buttoned firmly
round her, her keen eyes taking in every detail of the
place that she must know so well. Finally they rested
on the spotless sink and shining brass of the taps and
she remarked, 'You've got it all proper nice, Mrs

Ward.' She took off her coat and hung it behind the door, and Holly felt as if she had been awarded a good conduct mark.

'I couldn't do much about tidying up the garden,' she said apologetically to Mr Burkett, a large, slow-moving man with a placid face and huge, horny hands, and his wife answered for him,

'Oh, don't you fash yourself about that, m'dear. Joe'll soon put it all to rights.' She looked suspiciously towards the door into the hall. 'Now, where would that Mrs Kent be?'

Holly almost burst out laughing, but reminded herself in time that Blanche had been one of the reasons for the Burketts' earlier departure.

'Out for the day,' she said. Since Sam Robinson's appearance Blanche had returned to life with no trouble at all. Sam had appeared on Saturday morning, in a hired car, and taken Blanche out for the day. Dawn had transferred herself to Jared's car and they too had gone off somewhere together. The same programme had been followed on Sunday. Holly assured herself that she was pleased to have everyone out of the way so that she could prepare for the Burketts' arrival, but there were moments during the weekend of dusting and polishing and Hoovering when she bitterly regretted her promise to stay and reorganise the household for Jared.

'He's a selfish, odious beast,' she told Paws, who didn't seem in the least bit interested, 'and I'm fed up with this Cinderella act. If Mrs Burkett will stay and take over I'm going to change the pattern—and sharpish!'

And now Mrs Burkett was here and it looked as if she would stay. Holly showed her what was in the fridge and the freezer and they discussed meals, then

Mrs Burkett made a pot of tea and called Joe in from the garden, and they all drank tea together sitting round the kitchen table.

'You'll want to go and do some shopping this afternoon, Mrs Ward,' Mrs Burkett said, collecting the cups. 'I'll make a list for you. And how many will there be for dinner?' Holly felt firmly and politely excluded from the kitchen from then on.

The days that followed had a very odd feeling about them, and sometimes Holly stopped and asked herself what she was doing here. She shopped in Ambleside, and explored the little town with its winding straggles of shops and houses, all very grey and slatey. She looked in the shop windows at the beautiful bulky knitted coats and sweaters, but stopped herself from going inside and buying any of them. It was impossible to persuade herself that she would still be here to wear them in the winter, and they weren't the kind of clothes she would need in London. She walked alone over the fields and beside the lake and tried to keep her attention on the glorious scenery, but all she could think of was Jared and the way he had treated her. She wasn't in love with him, she couldn't be, but the sight of him made her heart race and just the sound of his voice gave her a hollow feeling inside.

Blanche spent all her days with the Robinsons, coming in flushed and happy in time for bed. Sam had hired a car and Holly gathered that they spent their time ancestor-hunting.

'I think it's lovely the way he wants to trace his family,' Blanche sighed to Holly. 'So warm and human. He's such a nice man, Holly.' She giggled like a schoolgirl. 'And do you know, I think he's quite taken with me!'

Holly didn't know whether Dawn accompanied them on their expeditions or not. She wondered whether Jared was taking time off to entertain her, but he didn't mention it and Holly wouldn't ask. She saw hardly anything of him during those days. He went out immediately after an early breakfast, merely saying that he wouldn't be in for dinner. Holly took care to be in bed before he came in. She wanted to talk to him, to ask him to arrange for her to take up her new work as his partner in the firm, but when she did see him he was silent and preoccupied. She would have to wait, but she wasn't going to wait long.

It was on the Friday evening that events began to move again. Holly had had a solitary dinner, served by Mrs Burkett in the dining room, and was sitting with her coffee in the drawing room, Paws happily purring on her knee, trying to interest herself in a film about elephants in the African jungle, when the door flew open and Jared appeared.

He switched off the TV without asking her permission and dropped into a chair, heaving an almighty sigh. 'Eureka! It's happened. I've won!'

Holly's eyes widened and her inside went down like a lift. Dawn had promised to marry him? She felt sick. 'What happened?' she croaked.

He threw out his arms. 'Oh boy, oh boy! Uncle Sam for ever! She's leaving—she's going back with him to the Great Open Spaces!'

The cat must have sensed Holly's tension and began kneading her skirt feverishly, sticking his claws through to her tights. She tipped him on to the floor and stood up and fiddled with the coffee tray. She didn't want Jared to see her face. She said, 'Would you be trying to tell me something, by any chance?'

'I thought I had. It's Blanche, of course. Blanche and Sam Robinson. She's going back with them in Concorde on Wednesday. Sam wants to show her his li'l ol' home in Texas.' He roared with laughter. 'And once she's seen his li'l ol' home in Texas I doubt if we shall be troubled with Blanche again. It's been worth all the effort I've put in recently.'

'Effort?' echoed Holly stupidly.

'Well, of course, didn't you notice?' He lay back in his chair, a self-satisfied smile on his lips. 'It's been hard going these last few days, but I had to arrange it somehow so that the two lovebirds were on their own, that's why I've been spending my time amusing Dawn and keeping her out of their way. I have to admit that the child became very tedious after a time, but it was worth it in the end. It worked like a charm.' He rubbed his hands together. 'Great, isn't it?'

Great? It was earth-shaking, tremendous, miraculous—he wasn't in love with Dawn, she bored him. It was like the sun coming out after a storm. Holly turned and looked down at him—his face softened by satisfaction, his grey eyes creased up in amusement, long lashes fanning out almost to his cheeks—and her stomach turned over.

'Is it?' she said faintly.

'Of course it is. Good lord, you don't think I relished the prospect of being saddled with Blanche here for good, do you?'

'I suppose not,' said Holly. He hadn't relished the prospect of being saddled with *her* for good either. She wondered suddenly if he were already planning some way to get rid of her, and the world went dark again. Panic struck her. Suddenly she knew that she couldn't bear to leave this place—and this man.

Heaven help her, she was in love with him, fathoms deep in love.

Sam and Dawn arrived next morning to collect Blanche; he was driving his hired car down to Heathrow and leaving it there. Blanche, in a wine-coloured suit and a short mink coat, looked radiant, like a bride, and Holly wondered why she should have all the luck. Sam Robinson was a nice man and he would make a good kind husband. Holly's eyes strayed to Jared, who was loading Blanche's luggage into the boot of the car, and wondered what sort of a husband he would make. She wasn't likely to find out.

Blanche kissed her effusively, enveloping her in a cloud of Chanel Number Five. 'Goodbye, Holly dear, you've been so sweet to me. I'm sorry we haven't time to get to know each other better. Do write to me if you feel lonely without poor darling Paul and I'll understand and write back. Such a tragedy!' she murmured, dabbing her eyes. 'Such a terrible tragedy!' She turned back to smile at Sam, who was waiting to help her into the car.

Dawn wound her arms round Jared's neck and kissed him lingeringly. 'You will come and visit with us, won't you, Jarry? Promise!'

Sam, beaming all over his broad face, shook hands with Holly and then with Jared, and got into the car. When it had disappeared down the drive, with hands waving from the windows, Jared turned back into the house and said with brisk satisfaction, 'Well, that's that. I'll get along to the office and get some work done at last.'

It was now or never. Holly took a quick breath and said, 'Will you take me with you? I'd like to get started.'

He stopped halfway across the hall and stared at her. 'You weren't serious, were you, about working there?'

Holly went on walking into the dining room and picked up the coffee jug. 'Of course I was. You said we were to be partners. I've got the domestic arrangements ticking over nicely. Mrs Burkett seems quite happy and willing to stay and she's terrifically competent. What shall I do with myself if I don't have a job?'

It was taking a risk, and she held her breath. Jared could so easily say, 'Run away and enjoy yourself somewhere else. You're a girl of independent means now,' and there wouldn't be much she could do about it. But he looked at her for a moment with narrowed eyes, taking in her emerald green pants-suit that made her slender legs look longer than ever, and the curving cap of smooth brown hair that framed her small face, and then said, 'You'd better put on something—er— quieter, if you're coming. We've got a lot of men around at the mill, and if they see someone looking like you wandering about there'll be a few snarl-ups in the machinery. Cut along and change, and be quick about it.'

Holly flew upstairs and pulled off her pants-suit and put on jeans and a navy-blue sweater—the 'quietest' clothes she had with her. Her cheeks were pink with excitement, her eyes sparkling. Jared had accepted her—she was going to stay and become part of his life. It was a start.

She tied back her hair with a red ribbon and dashed downstairs again. At the kitchen door she sang out, 'I'm going to the mill, Mrs Burkett. Don't bother about lunch for me.'

Jared was waiting for her, standing by the car. He opened the door and as their arms brushed Holly's stomach flipped over. She would have to fight this extravagant physical response to him, she told herself. As he drove off she looked out of the window and said composedly, 'What a beautiful morning!'

She felt him glance round at her and after a moment he said, 'Yes, isn't it?' mimicking her tone, except that there was laughter lurking beneath.

It *was* a beautiful morning. The air was soft and gentle and the sunlight turned the grass into a golden haze. Up in the mountains the cascading streams glittered like jewelled necklaces.

'You won't see many more days like this,' said Jared. 'Wait until the winter sets in, then you'll know about it. You'd better have a shopping expedition and buy yourself some warm clothes.'

'Yes, I will,' Holly said, and almost hugged herself as she imagined sitting with Jared in front of a huge log fire, with the snow falling outside. Talking about the business, perhaps. Further than that she wouldn't allow her imagination to take her.

The mill was about a mile away, down the valley, and it was much larger and more spread-out than Holly had expected. Banks of trees softened the lines of its huddle of white low buildings, and a river gushed and foamed beside the largest of them. Jared parked his car and led the way between two lorries that were being unloaded in the yard, stopping to have a word with the men who were doing the job. Then, at the side of one of the buildings, he opened a door marked, 'Enquiries' and grinned at Holly as he held it for her to go inside. 'Welcome to your inheritance, Mrs Ward,' he said dryly.

The following half-hour was a terrible let-down for Holly. She hadn't known what to expect of the mill, but certainly nothing as huge and complex and noisy as it proved to be. Clad in a white coat, with a cap protecting her hair, and ear-muffs protecting her ears from the din and clatter of the huge machines, she hurried after Jared from one area to another, getting more and more hopelessly bewildered every moment.

His pace never slackened and as they passed from one machine to the next he shouted words close to her ear which meant nothing to her—carding, combing, blending, crimping, slivers, staple—it was like a foreign language. The machines seemed to think for themselves in a way that fascinated but vaguely alarmed her—clattering and clanging and banging, as they rolled and cut and spun and wove, their steel arms reaching and stretching and swinging at precisely the right moment. Holly had a sudden vision of long-ago village women, sitting peacefully outside their cottage doors with their spindles, setting up their hand-looms, perhaps singing as they worked, the scent of honeysuckle and the song of birds in the air.

She brought her attention back to the workers here, in their biscuit-coloured boiler-suits, moving round swiftly and efficiently at their jobs. If they sang at their work it wouldn't be heard through their ear-muffs, and the only smell was a mixture of smells—sweet, acrid, oily, quite impossible to describe. They looked cheerful enough, though, and some of the women gave her curious glances as she passed and one or two of the men grinned at her. But it was obvious that their attention was on their work, not on the visitor being shown round by the boss. Nothing new about that, their glances seemed to say.

Holly began to feel very small and insignificant, and the astounding fact that apparently she owned half of this huge concern was even more impossible to comprehend than ever, now that she was seeing it for herself. 'What do you know about a textile mill?' Jared had asked her contemptuously, and she had airily announced that she could learn. What a hope!

By the time they moved on from the machine-shops and she was able to take off the ear-muffs her head was beginning to ache and she was ready to weep with disappointment.

This was better, though, she thought gratefully, as they passed from the noise and clatter to the comparative peace of large, light airy rooms where rolls of delicate material were being put through the stages of dying, printing and finishing, until there, suddenly, was the final product—the rolls and bales of material piled high on shelves and stacked upright in wooden frames.

'That's the lot,' said Jared, leading her into a rather untidy office, where a middle-aged woman in a white blouse was sitting before a typewriter at a side desk. 'Ah, Mrs Pennington.' Jared smiled at her. 'This is my sister-in-law, Mrs Ward, she's been on the Grand Tour and I'm sure she could do with some coffee.'

The woman was on her feet in a second, beaming at Holly. 'Certainly, Mr Kent. Two minutes.' The office door closed with a click behind her.

Jared waved Holly to a chair and sat down opposite, behind his littered desk. 'Well? Satisfied?' His grin was ironic.

'You knew, didn't you?' she said. 'You knew I'd never fit in here—that it would take a lifetime of work and study and experience before I could be of any use?' Her lip quivered. 'You just had to demonstrate the fact—to make me feel small?'

He leaned back in his chair, shaking his head. 'No, Holly, you're wrong. I merely think that heavy machinery isn't quite your thing.'

'Don't patronise me!' she snapped.

Their eyes met across the desk and locked together. 'And don't you always think the worst of me, my girl!' said Jared angrily.

Sudden antagonism flared between them, as Mrs Pennington came back into the office, bearing two mugs of coffee on a wooden tray. At a nod of thanks from Jared she put it down on the desk and went out of the office again.

'You haven't seen it all, of course,' said Jared, calming down, 'but I didn't think you'd be interested in the packing department or the office—such as it is.'

Holly met his eyes squarely; she wasn't quite defeated yet. 'On the contrary, I think that's where my interest might lie. Who does the marketing around here?'

He grimaced. 'I do at the moment—amongst other things. That was to have been Paul's side of things—my father's idea again. Our marketing manager had reached retiring age, but he stayed on for an extra year to teach Paul the job. But it didn't work out, of course. Paul was bone idle, for one thing, relying on his wonderful charisma to have the orders flowing in. It doesn't quite work like that. He was out in Mexico for six months and the result was one order. *One!*' He raised his eyes to the ceiling.

This was Holly's opportunity to stake out a claim for herself to be considered part of the company.

'And I got that order for him,' she said composedly.

'You may not know, but I was working for Paul in Mexico. I'd previously been working for the marketing manager of Greville Textiles.'

She didn't add—because he must surely know—that Greville Textiles was one of the largest textile companies in the country, and when Jared's dark brows went up she saw that he was impressed. She felt a spurt of triumph.

'Were you now? I didn't know that. You're full of surprises, Holly. Ambitious young woman, are you?'

'Very ambitious,' she said coolly. 'More so now than ever.'

His eyes moved lazily over her face. 'Why now? Because you find yourself suddenly rocketed to owning half of an old-established company?'

'No,' she said. 'Because the love-marriage-home-children thing has lost its appeal.'

'Oh, you never know—some bloke might come along——'

'No!' she said sharply, and then, more quietly, 'No, not again, thank you. The risk is too great.'

He nodded. 'I see,' he said seriously. 'I expect you're right.'

She had convinced him, she had saved her pride. She wished she could feel more satisfaction.

'But this puts a new complexion on the situation.' Jared was saying thoughtfully. 'We'll have to go into it in detail. Maybe I've got myself a real partner after all.' Suddenly he smiled at her—really smiled, his dark eyes friendly for the very first time—and her foolish heart lifted. 'Look, could you amuse yourself for an hour or so while I deal with a few things, then we could go into Ambleside and have a snack lunch and this afternoon I could show you some of our new designs and begin to put you in the picture. How does that appeal?'

Holly forgot about the noise of the machinery, about the ache that was fast disappearing from her head. 'Yes, I'd like that. Perhaps I could have another look at the store-room. I found that fascinating.' And she knew from Jared's expression that she had said the right thing.

The light was fading as Jared drove back to the house along the nearly-empty roads. As the car took the turn off the main road he pulled up, looking down into the valley. 'Well, there it is, what did you think of it?' he said.

Holly's eyes followed his to where the mill nestled in its cocoon of dark trees, the sunset touching the white spread of buildings with a rosy glow.

She said quietly, 'You love it, don't you?'

He turned back to her, startled. 'I suppose you might say that.'

'And yet you'd have put it all at risk—I found that out from the solicitor—just to get rid of me?'

He shook his head slowly. 'Not you, Holly. The girl Paul married—*any* girl. If he hadn't married, the whole of the company would have reverted to me, under my father's will. I could have gone ahead with all my plans to modernise, to put in new machines, new technology, expand the whole enterprise. And then I found I would have to share it all with some unknown female—that was too much to take. I think I went a little crazy at first.'

He turned to her and in the sunset light his face was hard as granite. 'Paul was bored here—dragging his feet. I thought I'd give him a chance to be useful and get him off my back for a while. I'd been in touch with Luis Ferida in Mexico and he thought there might be a market for our stuff out there, so I suggested that Paul should go out on a sales trip. He jumped at the chance and he left the following week—and just for good measure he took with him the girl I was going to marry.'

'Oh no!' breathed Holly but he didn't seem to hear. He went on as if he were talking to himself.

'I suppose it was my own fault. When you're in love with a girl as beautiful as Vivienne you shouldn't let her out of your sight, especially when there's a predator like Paul Ward around. But I was going through a tricky time at the office—there was a big contract hanging fire and I had to be backwards and forwards to London. I was keen to get it finalised so that we could fix the date of our wedding.' He added bleakly, 'I landed the contract—and lost my girl.'

Holly remembered then. The first time she had met Paul at Luis's house he had had a girl with him—a stunning brunette—the girl in the photograph.

'What happened?' she asked, when he didn't seem to be going to say any more.

He shrugged. 'They must have broken up pretty soon—as he married you. I never heard that she came home again. Her family lives a few miles along the valley, but we don't communicate much. For a long time I kept thinking she'd come back to me when she found out the kind of bloke that Paul was, but she didn't.'

'You'd have taken her back?' said Holly.

Jared looked at her in surprise. 'Of course,' he said. 'I loved her.'

He started up the engine and drove home without another word.

*   *   *

Holly and Jared had dinner together in the dining room—a wonderful steak-and-kidney pie, served by Mrs Burkett with due ceremony.

'Mrs Burkett's given us the full treatment.' Jared's eyes passed with amusement over the polished table with its lace mats and candles and posy of yellow chrysanthemums. 'She knows what's what, does our Mrs Burkett. She worked for Lady Something or other in Carlisle in the days of her youth, as she'll probably tell you, and she's a stickler for the "done thing".' He helped himself to another piece of pie and slanted a glance towards Holly as he added, 'I'm afraid she didn't approve at all of your late lamented husband's behaviour. Never mind, that's all water under the bridge now. I'm sure you'll get on very well with her, Holly.'

'I hope so,' Holly said rather shortly. Jared seemed to have forgotten completely their conversation in the car, but she hadn't.

At Jared's suggestion they took their coffee into the study. Mrs Burkett had lit a fire here and the small room looked cosy and lived-in. Jared settled down on the leather sofa and Holly looked around for somewhere else to sit, so that she wouldn't have to be so close to him. But there wasn't another chair in the room, except the one at the far side of the desk, and it would look rather ridiculous to go and sit over there. So she sat down beside him on the sofa, as far away as possible.

He leaned behind him to the desk and grabbed a large folder. 'Now, this is what I've had in mind to invest in. Kent and Son have to move with the times and use the man-made fibres, both alone and as mixtures. It's been all luxury trade so far, but we've got to widen our markets if we're to compete.' He opened the folder and pulled out a stack of glossy brochures, illustrating intricate-looking machines. 'Now this is what I have in mind——'

He talked machines until Holly's head felt like cotton-wool. She listened and tried to follow, but after the first few minutes she was lost and had to content herself with sitting quietly and watching the man beside her. He looked dynamic, vital, his grey eyes gleaming with enthusiasm for his plans. This was how he must have been at that other time, when he had Vivienne, his lost love, to work and plan for. What a fool she had been to leave a man like this for a weakling like Paul. What an utter and complete fool!

At last he seemed to notice her silence and turned to her with a wry smile. 'Am I boring the life out of you, Holly? It's just good to have someone to talk to—and of course I'll need your agreement if we're to go ahead. We're partners now, remember.'

She smiled back at him, loving him, trying not to look dreamy as her eyes fixed themselves on his face, as he bent forward with the folder on his knee. She saw the way his dark hair grew at his temples, the tiny lines around his eyes, the grooves beside his mouth——

It was as much as she could do not to lean towards him, to let her head rest against his shoulder. Instead she sat upright beside him and said, 'Of course I'm not bored—merely ignorant. Maybe I'll learn in time. But of course you have my agreement to anything that you think necessary. I trust your judgment absolutely.'

It was his turn to be silent now. He sat looking at her

with pure amazement in his face. At last he said wonderingly, 'I was so wrong about you, Holly. I've never been so mistaken in my life about anybody.'

There wasn't any reply to that. She had given him what he wanted; she hadn't been difficult or demanding; he was willing to accept her now. She supposed that was all she could expect.

She got to her feet because sitting so close to him was a torment. 'I'll go upstairs now,' she said, and added lamely, 'I'd like to—to wash my hair.'

Jared stood beside her and passed his hand gently over her mink-smooth hair. 'You have such pretty, soft hair,' he said.

She searched her mind wildly for some light reply, but all she could think of was 'Thank you', which would sound stupid.

He hesitated. 'O.K., go if you must,' he said. 'Goodnight, Holly, and thank you for everything.' He smiled down into her eyes, his long thick lashes nearly brushing his cheeks.

Holly's knees felt like elastic; she didn't know how she was going to get to the door. She was like a puppet, and someone was pulling a string that made her move the wrong way so that she nearly collided with the man beside her. His hand went out to steady her. Then, inevitably, his arms closed round her, pulling her towards him slowly.

She saw his mouth, only inches above her own. 'We seem to do something to each other, don't we?' he said, smiling. 'No need even to start a quarrel.'

She waited, aching, for his mouth to touch hers, and when it did she began to dissolve inside until she was all warm and soft and pliant, melting like wax under his hands. He sank down into the leather sofa without taking his mouth from hers and pulled her across his knee, cradling her legs with one strong arm while the other held her against him; kissing her as if he would draw every drop of sweetness from her mouth.

She let his hand go where it would; she wouldn't have stopped him then, she was lost in an ecstasy of pure feeling, powerless to resist, powerless to do anything but cling to him, her arms round his neck, her fingers in his hair, pulling, twining restlessly.

When he took his mouth away she moaned faintly, straining her body against his. Then she was dimly aware that he wasn't holding her any longer. He was straightening her legs on to the floor and sitting away from her, his head turned towards the doorway.

And in the doorway stood Mrs Burkett, her face stony, her mouth like a trap.

'I'm sorry, I'm sure, Mr Jared,' said Mrs Burkett in an icy voice. 'I did knock.'

Jared didn't lose his cool. 'That's O.K., Mrs Burkett, we didn't hear you. I'm afraid we were—er—otherwise engaged.' He grinned winningly, but the woman's face didn't relax its expression of stiff disapproval for an instant.

'I'll take the tray, then, if you've finished with it.' She even managed to make the harmless words sound like a rebuke. She took the coffee tray from the desk and departed, stiff and dignified, closing the door with a smart click.

Holly was trying to straighten her skirt, feeling sick with mortification. Jared stood up and poured himself a drink.

'Now we've done it!' he groaned, taking a swig. 'We're going to frighten her away again. She has her principles, has Mrs B.—That's why she left before.

Paul used to bring his girl-friends here and Mrs Burkett didn't approve of what they got up to.' His mouth twitched momentarily. 'Before she left she informed me that she wouldn't live in what she called a "disorderly house".'

He perched on the arm of the sofa and sat there in silence, frowning down into his glass. At last he said, 'We can't let Mrs B. go again, she's much too essential to our peace of mind. As far as I can see there's only one solution.'

Holly sat waiting. She couldn't believe that his solution—whatever it might be—was going to be anything other than unpleasant. 'Yes?' she prompted. She might as well know the worst straight away.

'I think the best thing, in the circumstances,' Jared said slowly, 'would be for us to get married.'

CHAPTER SEVEN

HE didn't mean to be unkind; he couldn't know that making a joke like that would hurt her so badly. Holly felt bruised inside as if she had walked straight into a jagged stone wall, but she managed to produce a fairly credible giggle because she was sure he was fooling. 'Tie the knot even more tightly, you mean?' she said. 'That would be rather a drastic step, wouldn't it?'

'I'm not joking,' said Jared, and she saw that he wasn't.

'But—but——' she spluttered.

'Now listen, Holly.' He took her hand as if she were a child, to be coaxed and reassured. 'It's a perfect solution. You notice I don't say anything about "love". You told me just now that you'd had enough of "love", and certainly I have too—Paul made sure of that for both of us. But there are other things. I need a wife. I need someone here to talk to, to entertain my friends. I need a woman in my bed—but I expect you've gathered that already,' he added drily.

The old trap! She felt cold creeping all through her as he went on talking. 'I need—I need—I need——' She had heard it before—from David—from Paul—and she had been thrilled and flattered, and then look where it had got her! No, she thought suddenly, not again. I won't fall for that line again. She would feel like a slave-girl, like a possession.

Her throat was dry and she got up and poured herself a drink, mostly water. Then she came back and sat down beside him. It was very strange, but now there was no longer the overwhelming urge to be held in his arms. She felt oddly remote from what was happening.

'And what about *my* needs?' she said quietly.

He smiled. 'Don't you think we've established what they are? You want me as much as I want you—go on, admit it. We'd be good together, you must know that.' His voice was a lazy, sexy drawl. His arm stretched along the back of the sofa behind her, but she moved away from it.

'Probably,' she said coolly. 'But I happen to believe that marriage means something more than being good together in bed. Of course that's important, but I'd want more than that from the man I married.'

He was still smiling, humouring her. 'Tell me,' he said, 'and I'll see if I can oblige.'

Holly leaned back in her corner and looked into his dark face and saw the arrogant confidence there. 'I can't put it into words,' she said slowly. 'All I know is that I should recognise it if it were offered.'

He had stopped smiling now. 'And I'm not offering it? Is that what you're saying?'

She bit her lip, nodding. 'I'm sorry, Jared.'

He stared moodily at her and she had a stab of remorse which she quickly fought down. Maybe she had hurt his pride by not jumping at his offer, but Jared wasn't a child to be given a sweetie to make the hurt better.

'Then we're back where we started,' he said, and breathed in hard through his nose, letting the breath out explosively.

'Certainly not,' said Holly firmly. 'We've agreed to be business partners, remember? I'm going to work for the firm on the marketing side. In everything else you'll have an absolutely free hand to run things any way you want. We could get Mr Windrush to draw up a legal document if you like—a power of attorney, or something. I'd take a salary—whatever you think the company could afford. You can go ahead with your plans to invest and modernise.'

Listening to her own cool, reasonable voice was like hearing someone else speaking. Perhaps she had changed into another girl, a different girl who had somehow become her own person and not a puppet on a string to be manipulated by a man for his own selfish needs.

'You seem to have it all worked out nice and tidy.' Jared got to his feet and started pacing up and down restlessly in the short space in front of the fireplace. He looked like a caged tiger. He was angry and disappointed. He'd been so pleased with his solution— so sure she would fall in with his plans, and now everything was going wrong. 'I'm sure you've solved the Mrs Burkett problem neatly too?' he said nastily.

'Oh, don't worry about Mrs Burkett,' Holly said with more confidence than she felt. 'I'll put things right with her. Anyway, it would be better if I didn't go on living here, now there's just the two of us. I'll go to a hotel in Ambleside for the moment, and begin to look round for a cottage for myself.'

He paused in his pacing and glowered down at her. 'Any more details you've planned? Do go on.' His voice was heavy with irony, his dark eyes glinting with anger.

She stood up and walked to the door, careful not to pass too near him. Her hand on the door-knob, she paused and said quite gently, 'It wouldn't have worked, Jared. You don't really want to be married to me, do you? This is a much better solution. And now I really will go up and wash my hair. I'll have a word with Mrs B. on the way up.' She opened the door and then turned back. 'Oh, I forgot to tell you. I spoke to Luis on the phone—he's coming to England some time soon and I invited him here to stay. He said he'd like to meet you. That O.K.?'

Jared stopped pacing and stood staring at her across the width of the small room. 'Luis?' he rapped out. And then, slowly, 'Ah yes, Luis. I see now.'

There was a short silence and then he picked up the machine catalogue from the desk and began to turn over its pages as if he had no further interest in the conversation.

'Is it O.K.?' Holly insisted. 'About Luis visiting, I mean?'

He half-raised his head, not meeting her eyes. 'Yes, of course,' he said absently. 'An excellent idea.'

Holly went out and closed the door. There was a long mirror in the hall and she straightened her dress and smoothed down her hair. Her face seemed surprisingly normal, considering that it was a different girl who looked back at her. There was, perhaps, a new self-possession about the tilt of her chin, a new firmness in the set of her lips.

She made straight for the kitchen, where Mrs Burkett was sitting bolt upright in a chair beside the Aga, knitting a grey sock. Paws was curled up on the rug at her feet and Mr Burkett was fast asleep in the opposite chair.

There was only one way to deal with this situation—head-on. Holly advanced into the kitchen, put one hand on the table, and said, 'Mrs Burkett, I'm sorry if you were embarrassed just now. I thought you would like to know that Mr Kent has asked me to marry him.'

She had said the right thing. Mrs Burkett's stiff back relaxed slightly and she put her knitting down on her lap. 'Well now, Mrs Ward, that's a different matter. A very sensible arrangement, if I may say so.'

'But of course it's much too soon,' Holly went on hastily. 'Nothing's finally decided yet, and I think the best thing will be for me to move out for the present. I shall go to a hotel in Ambleside tomorrow.'

Mrs Burkett nodded her approval. 'Very wise,' she observed. Her eyes turned towards her sleeping husband, his head lolling against the chair-back, his mouth hanging slackly open. 'Men,' announced Mrs Burkett repressively, 'don't always know where to draw the line. My grandmother used to say all men were wild beasts.'

Holly looked at the gently-snoring Mr Burkett—a docile and house-trained animal if ever she saw one—and smothered a giggle. 'I'll be moving out in the morning,' she said. 'I'm sure you'll look after things for Mr Kent very capably.'

Mrs Burkett picked up her knitting again. 'Oh aye, I expect we'll get along well enough.'

Holly walked to the door. 'I'll say goodnight then, Mrs Burkett.' She withdrew with a sigh of relief. Mrs Burkett would stay; her standards of propriety would not be outraged. Some, at least, of Jared's masculine needs would be satisfied. As for the rest of his needs— well, he could look for some other girl to supply them. There must be plenty who would jump at the chance. But not her—not the new Holly who wasn't going to fall for the third time when a man looked deep into her eyes and said he needed her. Oh no, not her. She had won an important trick tonight—several important tricks. But as she went slowly upstairs she wished she didn't have this heavy feeling that she had lost the game.

Next morning the sun was shining as she took the Mini out of the garage, and her spirits rose. Of course she hadn't lost the game, she just hadn't jumped the gun, that was all, and that was sensible. It would have been sheer madness to marry Jared. Feeling as she did about him her emotions would have been in a constant state of upheaval. She wouldn't have been able to concentrate on the work she had set herself or anything else.

Yes, she had done the right thing to refuse. She was still here, still working with Jared, seeing him every day. They had started off on the wrong foot with each other, but now it would be different. They would be colleagues—really get to know each other properly. And perhaps—in time—but she wouldn't let her plans take her any further.

The season was nearly over now and Holly booked in at a small family hotel in Ambleside without any difficulty. When she had unpacked in her pleasant room overlooking the lake, she drove out to the mill and made straight for Jared's office, her heart beating rather fast. She had purposely avoided him at breakfast and she didn't know how he would react to seeing her again.

She needn't have worried; he didn't react at all. He was alone in the office and he looked up from his desk with a brisk, 'Good morning, Holly. Everything fixed? Good. Then we can get ourselves organized. I've explained the position to Mrs Pennington and she's having a memo sent round to all the staff, defining your status in the company. You'll have no trouble, they're a friendly bunch.' He nodded towards a communicating door. 'Your office is in there—it's more or less as Paul left it. You'll want to sort things out, and then tomorrow we'll have a short managerial conference. I'll get the heads of departments in and we'll begin to plan our campaign. O.K.?'

'O.K.,' said Holly. Brisk and efficient—those were to be the keywords from now on. 'And what exactly *is* my position in the company?'

He pursed his lips, looking consideringly across the desk at her. 'How about "Marketing Director"? Or would you prefer "Partner"?' For the first time his lashes drooped and his eyes glinted with amusement. 'I can hardly call you a "sleeping partner", can I?'

Holly blinked and then she laughed lightly. If he wanted to make off-colour jokes she'd have to accept that as part of the equality she was claiming. She just hoped he wouldn't do it too often. Somehow she had to train herself to look upon him as a colleague for the time being—somehow she had to fight down the way her inside melted when their hands touched or she looked up and found his thick-lashed eyes fixed on her consideringly. 'Yes, "Marketing Director" will do fine. I'll put it on my door to give myself confidence.'

'Confidence—you? Don't give me that,' he scoffed, standing up and opening the door between the two offices. 'This is your own sanctum. How does it feel to be a Marketing Director?'

Her eyes passed round the office; the empty desk, the two phones, the filing cabinets, the house telephone—all the trappings of authority and responsibility, waiting for her, challenging her.

Quite suddenly she felt empty inside. Up to now she had tried to ignore the doubts that had been creeping up on her since she had taken that stand with Jared last night. But now they all descended on her together, like a flock of bats, wings beating in the darkness. She wanted to scream that it was crazy—of course she couldn't be a Marketing Director. Oh, she had a working knowledge of the job—two years with David Behrens had given that to her, enough to know that to be a good saleswoman you needed to know everything about the product you are selling.

That sale she had made in Mexico—it was probably Juanita's doing as much as hers. Juanita had been sorry for her after the David thing; she had wanted to help, to boost her confidence.

She panicked. 'This is ridiculous! I can't—I can't take on the job. I should never have said I could.' She hung on to the edge of the desk. She was shaking all over; tears were blinding her eyes. 'I—I'm sorry——' she gulped.

Jared's hand was on her arm, gripping it hard. 'Steady on,' he said. 'Easy does it. Come and sit down.' He led her round the desk and lowered her into the big executive chair on the far side of it. Then he stood back grinning.

'There,' he said. 'You look at home already. You look every inch the young woman executive.' His glance passed over her trim figure in the black suit and white blouse she had put on this morning—the only suitable clothes she could find; at this moment they seemed suitable for a funeral—hers.

He sat on the edge of the desk, swinging one long

leg easily. 'Look, Holly,' he said, 'nobody's expecting miracles. You and I are going to work together until you feel confident to take decisions alone. You didn't think I was going to leave you to cope, did you?'

She shook her head, biting her lip, feeling as if the big chair were swallowing her up. That was just what she *had* thought. 'Thank you, Jared,' she said. He was being generous and—and *nice*. He could have left her to make such a mess of everything that she had to admit failure; he could have taunted her with conceit, with her lofty claim that she could pull her weight in the company but instead he was going to help her. She felt as if she didn't know him at all.

She smiled a watery smile. 'Thank you, Jared. I'll do my best.'

He leaned forward and put an arm round her shoulders and dropped a brotherly kiss on her hair. 'That's my girl,' he said. 'Always a good little fighter. I'll leave you to find your way round. Good luck—and if you need help I'm here.' He went back into his own office and closed the door.

Holly sat staring blindly in front of her, fighting the turmoil rising inside. It was no use trying to fool herself any longer. It wasn't just that she fancied Jared so that his look, his touch, turned her bones to water. It was so much more than that. She had fallen in love with him, so deep in love that she was terrified, because he wasn't in love with her. It was going to be agony and fear working near him and not letting him see it. Being merely a colleague and partner when she might have been his wife.

In the next weeks Holly began to get a feeling for the job. Kent and Son was a family firm, highly specialised and catering for the luxury side of the trade. Very different from the huge national concern that she had worked for previously, but her experience there proved invaluable now. She had something to thank David Behrens for after all.

She made a start at unscrambling the muddle that Paul had made of the paper work. She found out who the reps were and which areas they covered. She met one of them, Peter Benson, a charming middle-aged man with a winning smile, who produced snapshots of his wife and children when they lunched together in Ambleside. She liked that—she guessed that he started that way with any woman he met on his travels round the country.

'I liked Peter Benson,' she told Jared later on, when they were discussing his order book. 'Straightforward type.'

'Huh!' He slanted her a sceptical glance. 'Straight for the target, you mean, don't you? You'd better watch it, young Holly.'

'I can deal with Peter Benson and his ilk,' she grinned. And then she saw Jared's eyebrows lift and knew he was thinking the thought that had just occurred to her too—that she hadn't been noticeably successful in dealing with Paul. 'I've changed,' she said a trifle defensively.

He looked at her quizzically. 'Don't change too much,' he said softly. 'I rather liked you as you were.'

She laughed that off as casually as he had said it. He hadn't liked her at all—he'd hated her; hated her for barging in—a total stranger—and disrupting all his plans.

But she hadn't, in the end, disrupted his plans and he didn't hate her now, she was sure of that. He had accepted her. He was unfailingly helpful. He never got irritated or angry when she interrupted him to clear up some point in the order book or the invoices, or to ask about new designs or samples or a hundred and one other things.

She had to resist the temptation to make up difficulties just for the joy of going into his office and seeing him raise his head from his work and say, 'Hullo, what can I do for you?' and smile at her under his fabulous lashes.

His smile was like a drug that she was becoming addicted to. It made her feel warm and happy and secure.

She tried not to read too much into it. Of course he would want her to learn everything as quickly as possible. He'd accepted the fact that he was stuck with her, so it would be only common sense to encourage her and give her confidence so that she could pull her weight and be really useful to him as quickly as possible, and she turned to him constantly.

She was a quick learner. She took books and papers back to the hotel and worked on them in the evenings. But being a woman executive was a new role, and she was constantly being faced with new situations and decisions. The worst thing was that she couldn't afford to let anyone see that she often felt confused and frightened.

Only Jared knew, she didn't try to hide it from him—and anyway she couldn't have done. She had the feeling that behind those watchful grey eyes was a computer working away, registering every thought in her head. Sometimes it terrified her, in case he knew how she really felt about him. That would spoil everything, most of all the friendship that was developing between them.

Her days were filled with interest. When she had worked for David Behrens it had been in the office entirely—the manufacturing side of the business was spread around the country. But here it was all packaged together, she could see the whole process from beginning to end. The factory manager, Bert Gregg, a redheaded wiry little man, was a mine of information. He seemed to like her and was obviously pleased by her interest and the continual questions she shot at him. Sometimes she donned overalls and went into the machine-shops and watched, fascinated, as the bales of filament went through all their different processes, to emerge finally as the exquisite materials that would finally be fashioned into evening gowns, cocktail dresses, blouses, scarves, curtains, bedcovers— She went often into the sales room where the finished fabrics hung from circular stands, and ran her fingers luxuriously over the materials, plain or textured, sheer or nobbly, glossy or matt, in muted plain colours or vibrant, rich patterns. On her desk were piles of fashion magazines that seemed to her to link everything up, and although she would have no part in the designing and making of the final articles she felt that she was forming a small part of a long, fascinating chain.

She discovered that the designs were the work of an artist who lived in one of the nearby villages, and one of the first things that Holly did was to visit her. Tessa Black was a tall angular young woman who lived alone in a cottage with a tangle of garden and a wonderful view over the fells.

Holly got on well with Tessa from the start. She was a practical Northener—no nonsense about Tessa. She brewed coffee in the big garden studio and looked Holly up and down in a friendly manner.

'So you're Kent's new marketing wizard? You've arrived just in time. Jared's been working himself towards an early grave just lately.'

Holly hadn't thought of it like that, but now she did. She was beginning to realise what it meant to run a mill—even a smallish mill like Kent's—almost singlehanded, as Jared did.

She nodded seriously. 'I want to learn quickly,' she said. 'My previous experience doesn't give me all I need here. I've got dozens of questions I want to ask you.'

'Ask away,' said Tessa amiably.

Holly stayed all afternoon and left with a notebook crammed with information about colours and designs, about the lines that were being discontinued and the new ones that were in the planning stage. Tessa was a real professional—she didn't stop at producing the beautiful designs that were the hallmark of Kent materials, she was a mine of information about the materials themselves and their composition, even about technical problems concerned with printing and finishing. Holly left with a feeling that she had taken a big step forward and that, even more important, she had made a friend. Tessa hadn't spoken directly about Paul, but it was plain that she had known him and knew the situation and was being tactful.

'Come whenever you feel like it.' Tessa stood at the door of the studio as Holly climbed into the Mini. 'I hang up a Don't Disturb notice when I'm working, but just ignore that. You're one of the team.'

One of the team—it felt good. It felt doubly good to be working so close to Jared. He brought her in on everything that went on, introduced her to customers—the local ones who called at the office, and the ones farther afield in the areas not covered by one of the three reps. He took her with him when he drove to see buyers even as far away as Manchester and Liverpool.

They talked easily on the journeys—usually about the job, but sometimes a companionable silence fell and then Holly had the warm, satisfied feeling that something was growing and developing between them, a closeness, an understanding. When she said goodnight to the 'permanents' in the hotel lounge and went up to her bedroom, tired with the day's pressure of work, she would lie awake for a while and hug to herself the dream that was fast becoming more and more of a possibility—that one day before long Jared would suggest marriage again. And this time she would say yes, even if he didn't offer 'love'.

She worried a little about Paws, but Jared assured her that he was well and happy and getting sleek and even portly. 'Mrs Burkett seems to have taken a fancy to him,' he said. 'He's a star mouser—probably the result of a deprived childhood.'

Holly thought he might have said, 'Why don't you come up to the house and have dinner and then you can see for yourself?' but he didn't, and she didn't suggest it. Once or twice they had dinner together, when they had been working late, but it was always the same hotel that Jared took her to—the one where they had first dined together, where they had met Sam Robinson and Dawn.

That seemed years ago, in another life, when Jared had been hating and resenting her, and she didn't want to remember it. It brought it all back one morning when he said, 'I had a phone call from

Houston last night. Blanche and Sam Robinson are getting hitched—what did I tell you? We're invited to the wedding—want to go?'

Holly laughed. 'No thanks. Please make my apologies. Are you going?'

'Not on your life! Blanche is much more bearable at a distance. We'd better send them a present—can I leave that to you?'

Holly agreed and Jared pulled out a folder and said, 'Now, about this order of Frenton's——' And that was the end of Blanche, as far as he was concerned.

In November the weather struck a rough patch and Holly got her first taste of Lakeland rain. It rained for days, sheeting across the lake and the fells, the tops of the mountains hidden in thick mist from first light to early dark. The 'permanents' at the hotel clustered round a roaring fire and thought Holly was very plucky, the way she tackled the streaming roads in the little Mini every day. They had probably forgotten what it was to feel young and full of vitality, as Holly did these days. She had found a knitwear factory in Ambleside that made and sold beautiful knitwear, and stocked up with a zestful collection of jackets and jumpers in background shades of mink—to tone with her hair—patterned in Fair Isle with gorgeous mixtures of burnt orange, rust, poppy, flamingo.

She had slight reservations the first time she wore one of her new treasures at the office. 'Do I look—er— suitable?' she asked Jared doubtfully.

He put both hands on her shoulders and turned her round, then held her at arm's length and said, 'You look—fabulous, lovey. Good enough to eat.' He stroked the fuzzy texture of the wool. 'Maybe for a goat, anyway,' he laughed.

He went on holding her, smiling down into her eyes. Then suddenly the smile disappeared and they both went quiet. The sound of the machines in the distance seemed to die away and Holly stood holding her breath, her heart beating unevenly.

Jared muttered something under his breath, then he bent his head and kissed her, holding her tightly against him, every muscle taut and straining, a kiss like Holly had never known, a kiss throbbing with longing and desperation, that scorched and burned like a flame.

She had no awareness of time passing. She was oblivious of everything but the blood beating through her body as his mouth ravaged hers. She didn't even know whether she responded or not; while they clung together, mouth to mouth, she was in another world, a world of pure sensual ecstasy that was a revelation. Nothing that had happened before in her life had prepared her for this. When he let her go and moved away she was pale and shaking.

He walked over to the window and looked out to where the rain was still gushing down across the yard outside. 'If I did what I should I'd go out and take a walk across the fells and cool down,' he said moodily.

Then he came back and stood on the opposite side of the desk. 'I won't say I'm sorry, because I'm not.'

She gave him a fleeting smile. 'Forget it,' she said, trying to sound ordinary. A kiss was nothing in an office—it happened frequently, she told herself. Oh, but that kiss wasn't nothing, it was no use pretending.

He said, 'Dinner tonight? We'll drive out somewhere down the valley—have a change.'

She said, 'I'd like that.'

'Good. That's a promise.' His voice was husky, his

eyes told her what his words weren't saying.

There was an odd little silence, then he shook his shoulders and said, 'Now then, to work.' He pressed a button on the intercom. 'Mrs Pennington, have you got the diary, bring it in, will you?'

The rain didn't let up and by ten o'clock Jared was fuming. 'Why the hell did I arrange to go up to Penrith to see Slater this morning? The roads will be awash, I'll have to go slow. I can't phone and back out, he's a touchy devil and we don't want to lose him—that's quite a sizeable order he's promised. We've got this man from Duncan's coming in at two, haven't we? He's always a real tough nut to crack, but if we can get him interested in the two new lines—you know, these two——' he flicked over a pile of swatches on the desk '——it would be a real triumph. I'll be back in time to see him, never fear. If I'm a few minutes late you'll hold the fort, Holly? Give him your sweetest smile,' he grinned. 'Soften him up.'

Holly grinned back. 'Will do.' She felt light and floating, she wanted to sing and dance around the office and do something really crazy. Tonight she was going out with Jared and this time they wouldn't be talking business.

It was a busy day. Jared, who'd had trouble getting round a flooded road, was late getting back for his appointment and Holly had to practise her new sales technique on the man from Duncan's. Perhaps because she was riding high on cloud nine, she thought afterwards, she managed to clinch a sizeable order which had been hanging in the balance for several weeks.

She couldn't wait to announce her success to Jared when he finally returned. 'No!' he exclaimed, staring unbelievingly at the signature on the order form. 'Truly?'

Her brown eyes were dancing as she nodded. 'You didn't think I could, did you? You thought I'd be a drag.' She wanted to hear him deny it, to say he was glad to have her working with him.

His long lashes drooped, hiding his eyes. 'Fishing, are we? O.K., for the record, I think you're a bloody marvel. Now we'll have two things to celebrate tonight.'

She didn't dare to ask him what the second thing was, in case she was wrong. But she was almost sure she knew, and there was a warm stirring inside as she let the hope grow into a near-certainty.

It was well after six when they finished work and the office was empty, except for the two of them. 'Hungry?' enquired Jared, and Holly admitted to being famished.

'We're going up to Keswick,' he said. 'A good place I know there, a bit off the beaten track. I booked on the way back this morning.'

Holly's breathing quickened. *Booked.* Did he mean booked a table for dinner or was he planning to stay the night?

'Did you know you left one of your cases behind at Glenthorpe—a small one?' he said casually. 'I stuck it in the back of the car, I thought you might need it.'

Now there was no doubt what was in his mind. No doubt in her mind either; this was the man for her and she couldn't deny her heart any longer. She looked at him as he pushed the papers on his desk together, dark and lean and crackling with vitality, and felt weak with longing.

'Thanks, that was a good idea,' she said lightly. 'It might save me going back to the hotel to change. Will you bring it in, please, and I'll see what I can find to wear.'

It proved to be packed with reminders of the days in Mexico—clothes that she felt had a jinx on them and that she had not expected to wear again, but for tonight she felt confident enough to put the past behind her. In the cloakroom she opened the case and looked through the contents. Something soft and romantic—she felt unashamedly romantic tonight; the image of the successful business women had been established today. Jared had accepted her as colleague and partner. But tonight would be something different.

She chose a pretty georgette blouse with full, gathered sleeves in grape colour with a darker velvet skirt clipped in round her small waist with a cummerbund sash. It would be damp underfoot and she could change her tights and shoes when they arrived. As she slung her coat round her she felt excitement rising inside her like bubbles in champagne—it was going to be a wonderful, wonderful evening.

She chattered all the way to Keswick in the car, about the tourist attractions in Ambleside that she had made time to see; about the old dears who were residents at her hotel; about Tessa and her studio; about anything that came into her head, because she knew if she stopped talking there would be silence between them and the tension would mount and she would snuggle up against him because his nearness was driving her wild. And that wouldn't do because he might—he just *might*—be thinking of this dinner merely as a celebration of the important order she had landed by herself. She couldn't risk taking him for granted.

The hotel was a small local gem—soft lighting, thick black beams, whitewashed walls, and carpets that your feet sank into. A log fire burned in the inglenook of the entrance hall and an enormous black setter was stretched out on a rug before it. Jared carried her case in and left her at the door of the ladies' powder-room.

'I'll see you in the bar when you're ready.' He put his hand on her arm and a ripple of excitement passed through her at his touch, so that when she got inside the room she had to sit down on one of the pink brocade stools until she steadied up.

She opened her case and smoothed a pair of gossamer-thin tights over her slim legs, stroking them slowly, a little smile on her lips. Her sandals were black suede with very high heels and thin straps and her skirt swished softly round her knees as she sat to put them on. She shivered. She had never before felt so expectant, so sensuously warm and aware. It was frightening.

She sat at the mirror to do her face. The powder-room was all pale shell-pink, even the lights over the mirror. Very flattering! She had always had a good skin, but the weeks in the soft air of the Lakes had made it even more delicately perfect. She needed just a touch of make-up and concentrated on her eyes. A pearly-brown shadow and lots of mascara tonight! Her hand was shaking as she wielded the tiny brush.

Behind her she heard the door open and two women came into the room. Holly glanced in the mirror and saw that one of them was tall and matronly with blue-rinsed hair. She was speaking under her breath, but she had the kind of voice that carries across vast distances with no effort at all.

'My dear girl,' she was saying, with more than a

tinge of impatience, 'you really are being rather silly. Why don't you just do as I say?'

A higher, lighter voice replied nervously, 'I can't, Mother, really I can't. I should feel dreadful.'

'Rubbish! You'll have to face him some time, and it may not be nearly as bad as you think. Just go up and say hullo as if nothing had happened. He's sitting in the bar and he's obviously on his own.'

The door of one of the cubicles opened and closed again. Holly replaced the brush in the mascara case carefully. It couldn't be, of course, she was just being super-sensitive, but suddenly the warm, scented room felt chilly.

There was a long sigh from somewhere behind her and then a face appeared in the mirror next to hers, framed in a collar of white fur. The face of the girl in the photograph. A white, trembling hand went up to push back a wisp of raven-black hair. A pair of huge violet eyes met hers in the mirror and the girl gave her a shy, fleeting smile and looked away again quickly.

A water-flush sounded, the cubicle door opened again and the older woman came out. 'Ready, Vivienne? Now, be sensible and go and speak to him straight away before you have time to think about it. It may be ages until you get another chance. Daddy and I will wait in the car.' The door of the cloakroom swished to after them.

Holly stared at her own stricken face in the mirror. 'No,' she whispered. 'Oh, no!' But even as she said it she knew that the worst possible thing had happened.

Vivienne, the girl that Jared loved, had come back.

CHAPTER EIGHT

HOLLY sat very still, her fingernails digging into her palms, her breathing shallow. Then she stood up and walked stiffly to the door. She must see Jared's face when the girl greeted him. She had to know for sure.

The ladies' powder-room was at the end of a passage leading to the reception hall, and the door of the bar led off the hall. The two women were disappearing through that door as Holly emerged into the passage and she hurried after them. The bar was brightly lit and full of people and the warmth and chatter and clink of glasses met her as she reached the door.

Jared was sitting on a high stool, a drink in front of him, talking to the barman. As Holly stopped just inside the door, half hidden by a group of men holding glasses and laughing convivially, her heart squeezed up at the sight of him, of his strong, dark face, and hard, magnificently-fit body in the dark trousers and silky grey-striped shirt he was wearing. She loved him quite desperately and she was terribly afraid she was going to lose him for good.

The two women walked to a table at the side of the room where a thickset man with greying hair was sitting. He got up as they approached and after a moment he and the older woman prepared to leave. The girl stood a little apart from them, twisting her hands together. Oh, but she was beautiful, even more beautiful than her photograph had shown. Straight, pure black hair, pale, translucent skin, high cheekbones throwing faint shadows beneath, a soft, vulnerable mouth. She was wearing a short white fur bolero over a black crêpe dress, and high suede boots, and she stood out among the other women in the bar like a fragile harebell in a bed of hardy annuals.

Her parents were leaving now. Holly drew back as they passed her, the woman sweeping through the doorway with a backward nod of encouragement to the girl who stood hesitating still.

At last she straightened her shoulders slightly and moved forward towards Jared, at the bar, standing a little behind him. Her back was towards Holly now, but the girl must have spoken, for Jared spun round on his stool. As he recognised her his frown of surprise changed slowly to a smile of such blazing delight that Holly and to look away for a moment. When she turned back Jared had pulled up another stool and was listening, nodding now and then, intent on the girl beside him and what she was saying. At one point she put a delicate white hand timidly on his arm and he leaned towards her, covering her hand with his.

Holly winced as if she had suffered a mortal wound. She had seen enough. Turning away, she pushed behind the group of businessmen and walked slowly back to the cloakroom. 'Would you have taken her back?' she had asked him, and he had said, simply, 'I loved her.'

Now he had her back, his lost love, and where did that leave Holly? She and Jared were still bound together by that fatal knot that his father had tied. Somehow it would have to be cut. There would be no place for her here when Jared was married to Vivienne.

Her dressing case lay open on the floor in the cloakroom, where she had left it. Clumsily, her hands stiff and cold, she secured the locks and carried it to the receptionist. 'May I leave this with you for a while?' she asked the girl. 'I haven't got the keys of the car.'

'Certainly, madam.' The girl looked curiously at her as she took the case and put it behind the desk. 'Are you dining?'

'Yes—no—I'm not quite sure.' Holly wasn't sure of anything at the moment. She wanted to hide herself somewhere, but there was no way she could do that. She didn't know what was going to happen next, all she could do was to wait and somehow manage to get through the next few minutes, one at a time.

There was a small residents' lounge on the opposite side of the hall from the bar, and it was empty. She wandered in there and picked up a magazine and bent her head over it. She knew she was in a state of shock; her heart was beating unevenly, her skin was icy cold, she was having difficulty with breathing. Somehow she must pull herself together before she faced Jared and that girl.

Then she heard voices in the hall, just outside the door. 'Tomorrow, then?' the girl's voice came to her, light and eager. 'It'll be such fun, darling, we've got so much to catch up on——'

They were getting further away now. Holly heard Jared's deep voice say, 'Tomorrow—I'll look forward——' And then they passed on and she could hear no more.

She went out into the reception hall and waited for Jared to come back. He was smiling as he approached her from the big entrance door. 'Ah, there you are, Holly. I've got a drink waiting for you, come along.'

He linked his arm in hers and led her back into the bar, and she sat on the stool where Vivienne had been sitting a minute or two previously and sipped the drink that was put in front of her. It caught at her dry throat and made her cough.

She took an olive from the dish that Jared pushed towards her. She thought she would never taste the astringent bitterness of an olive again without remembering this moment of misery.

He helped himself to a couple of crisps and munched them with relish. 'You know, an extraordinary thing's just happened. Vivienne's back—you know, the girl I was engaged to once upon a time. She came up and spoke to me.'

'I know,' said Holly. 'She was in the ladies' room with her mother. I recognised her from a photo I'd seen in your study. It fell out of a drawer when I was looking up a phone number.'

She might have saved herself the trouble of explaining; Jared wasn't listening. 'She's more beautiful than ever,' he said in a bemused voice. 'Fantastic, isn't she?'

Holly nodded. 'Yes.'

Ha laughed, shaking his head. 'Would you believe it, she said she was scared to speak to me! She thought I might play the heavy betrayed lover, I suppose. A good thing we don't still live in the days of Victorian melodrama. We take things as they come now.'

'Yes,' said Holly again.

He slid off his stool and held out a hand to her. 'Come along, let's eat. I'm famished, aren't you?'

She saw that he was doing his best to behave as if nothing important had happened, as if he had been pleased to meet an old friend, and that was all, and she had to take her cue from him.

But something important *had* happened, and they both knew it. The atmosphere between them had changed completely. Over dinner there were no intimate glances, no long silences that promised unspoken delights. If Jared had intended to ask Holly again to marry him; if he had meant them to spend the night here together, then Vivienne's appearance had changed all that. Well, it would, wouldn't it? Holly thought miserably.

Over dinner they talked about the order Holly had got from Duncan's that afternoon. They discussed prices and delivery dates and Tessa's new idea for a headscarf design, and Jared spoke about his meeting this morning in Penrith. They were business colleagues—partners—and that was all. It was odd, Holly thought, how you could go on talking and smiling and be slowly dying inside. She had no idea what they ate; she just hoped her stomach would receive it without rebellion. It would be awful if she had to rush away and be sick. She was very careful about the amount of wine she drank, just taking a sip occasionally. Usually Jared was punctilious about keeping her glass filled, but this evening he wasn't noticing. She thought, We're like two indifferent actors, mouthing through our parts out of habit, with our thoughts hundreds of miles away.

They had coffee at their table. Holly had hers black and it helped to steady her. She drained her cup to the last drop and turned to him. 'Thank you, Jared, that was a lovely dinner, but I'd like to be getting back to my hotel now if that's all right with you. I've got some work there that I want to get finished for tomorrow. I left my case with the receptionist—will you put in in the car, please? And ask for my coat?'

He stood up, frowning, looking down at her with an odd, unreadable expression on his face. 'I got it wrong, then, did I?' he said wryly.

She didn't pretend to misunderstand. She said in a calm little voice, 'Perhaps we both got it wrong, Jared. And everything's different now, isn't it? Please take me back.'

'If that's what you want.'

'It is,' she said, and she could almost feel his relief as she turned and walked out of the restaurant ahead of him, her chin lifted, her back very straight. All had been said that needed to be said, without any words at all. She hadn't made a fool of herself, but the thought gave her no satisfaction, and there was ice in her veins where warm blood should be.

It was raining again when the car pulled up outside Holly's hotel in Ambleside. They had exchanged only a couple of remarks on the drive back—about the weather. 'You left the Mini at the mill,' Jared said now. 'I'll pick you up tomorrow morning about half-eight. O.K.?'

'Thanks,' said Holly. 'No, don't get out, I'll see myself in—it's pouring with rain. Goodnight, Jared, and thanks again for my dinner.' She slid out of the car, clutching her coat round her, and ran up the steps. She heard the car drive away before she reached the door.

A week crawled past and on the surface nothing had changed. Holly was needing Jared's advice less now and she didn't ask for help unless she was desperate. When it was absolutely necessary to discuss anything they discussed it amicably. They were still colleagues—partners—but the vital spark had gone out of their relationship.

Holly felt as if she were living on the edge of a precipice. The days were bearable—she kept herself busy; it was the evenings that were the worst. She had no heart, now, for taking books and papers back to work on. She sat with the residents in front of the TV and stared blindly at the screen, wondering where Jared was and if he was with Vivienne and what they were doing. It wasn't quite time yet, but soon, she was certain, he would tell her that he and Vivienne were going to be married, and she knew that somehow, when that happened, she must get away.

But how? Where to? She and Jared were still tied by that absurd knot that bound them together as partners in the business. Could she possibly stay and make a life for herself here and watch his happiness with another woman? It would be torture.

She stayed late on Friday evening, postponing the moment when she would have to go back to the hotel and make pleasant conversation. At half-past six the phone rang in Jared's office. He would have left by now and Holly went through to answer it. But Jared hadn't left, he was sitting at his desk and as Holly opened the door he held the receiver to her. 'It's for you,' he said. 'Luis Ferida.'

She took the phone from him. 'Luis—how lovely to hear from you! Are you in England—are you coming up here?' Warmth spilled into her voice, her eyes lit up eagerly. Luis had been such a rock in time of trouble before; somehow he seemed to promise a way out now.

'No, I am not in England, 'Olly. I 'ave not been able

to get away yet. I ring from my office. It is morning here and the sun is shining. 'Ow is it with you?'

She chuckled, imagining Luis's monkey face, his quiet little grin. 'It's nearly dark and raining. We're celebrated for our rain here.' She caught a glimpse of Jared's expressionless face as he pushed his papers together on the desk. 'Is it business, Luis?'

'Yes, it is business, my dear 'Olly. I have written to Mr Kent, but I telephone as well because I think it is important that someone from England come out here, with lots and lots of fabric samples and everything— 'ow do you say it—genned up for selling. There is great interest being shown here in your products, after that sale you made to Casa Angela—you remember? I think the market expands for Kent and Son, heh? What do you day, 'Olly, will you come yourself? You could stay with Juanita—she talks of you so often—she would be delighted.' A little pause. 'And I should be delighted too.'

It was like a door opening in a dark cell, letting in the light. Holly sank into a chair, pressing the receiver to her ear. 'Oh, Luis, how marvellous, and what a lovely idea! I really don't see why I shouldn't. Look, I'll talk it over with Jared—with Mr Kent—and see what we can arrange. I'll ring you back tomorrow about this time—how would that be?'

Luis slipped into Spanish, as he did when he was pleased and excited. '*Bueno. Esto es maravilloso. Le veremos otra vez pronto?*'

'*Sí, creo que sí. Adios, Luis.*' She replaced the receiver, smiling.

'Quite the linguist, aren't we?' said Jared, with an edge to his voice.

'I did an A-level course in Spanish before I went

out to Mexico,' she said, refusing to be needled. 'Enough to get around out there.'

'H'm.' He tucked his briefcase under his arm. 'What did he want?'

Holly told him everything that Luis had said—well, nearly everything. 'I think I should go,' she said. She was a partner, she didn't have to ask permission. 'It looks as if we might be on to a good thing. I could do a bit of travelling around while I'm there—research in other towns. Mexico's economy may be rocky, but there's plenty of money about still for luxury goods.'

He was looking hard at her. 'You want to go?'

Holly smiled brilliantly. 'Oh *yes*, I'd love to. I'd like to see Luis and Juanita again too. They're such good friends.'

'Of course,' Jared said drily. 'Well, it's up to you, of course. When will you go?'

She appeared to consider, but actually her thoughts had run ahead. This might be her way out. This was a wonderful opportunity to get away, and once she was thousands of miles away she could start to make some plan to extricate herself from the position she was in here. Certainly she would work it so that she needn't come back to England for a long time. 'Oh, as soon as possible,' she said. 'As soon as I can put things together. And, Jared, don't you think it might be a good idea to take on another member of staff on the marketing side? We need to concentrate on export now—we agreed that, didn't we?—and if I do the travelling we shall need someone here to help you while I'm away.'

His face was expressionless. 'I'd need notice of that. We'll talk about it again when you get back from Mexico.'

'O.K.,' she said. She wasn't going to come back, not for a very long time, but she had made the suggestion, she needn't do any more. 'Well, I'll be off, then. See you in the morning.'

She had reached the door before he said sharply, 'Holly!'

'Yes?' She turned, smiling.

He came round the desk towards her. 'Holly, we need to talk. If you're going away for a time——' He thrust his hands deep into his pockets. 'Look, it's about Vivienne—you know the position. I think you two ought to meet. I know it might seem awkward— the situation between you is somewhat unusual.' He smiled bleakly. 'Paul left two widows, in a way. But she and her parents live so near, there's no need for a feud to develop.'

Holly shook her head. 'There's no feud as far as I'm concerned, Jared, and some time I'd like to meet Vivienne. We could compare notes, couldn't we?' she added with a brittle little laugh.

His mouth tightened and he frowned down at her. 'That's not like you, Holly. I don't seem to know you lately.'

'Perhaps you never did,' she said brightly. 'Now, I really must go, I've got a lot to think about—clothes and so on. We'll fix a date to meet when I get back, O.K.?'

'Whatever you say.' She heard the anger in his voice, saw it in his face.

She wasn't going to stop to quarrel with him. 'Goodnight, Jared,' she said, and went swiftly out of the office.

After dinner at the hotel she went up to her room. It wouldn't take her long to pack—she had decided to buy a new outfit or two when she got to Mexico; it would do her good, she decided, to start from scratch and not go on wearing the same clothes. They were still almost new, most of them, but they held too many memories. And the chunky hand-knitted coats and tops she had bought here would certainly not be appropriate for Mexico's warm days. Even in the cool evenings she wouldn't need thick Fair Isle sweaters.

She was doing her best to narrow down her attention to clothes when the phone rang beside her bed. The manager's voice said, 'Mrs Ward? There's a lady at Reception would like a word with you. Can you come down?'

A lady? It must be Tessa; she had called in once or twice before in the evening. Holly ran downstairs, pleased at the opportunity of having a chat with Tessa and telling her that she was going to Mexico.

But it wasn't Tessa. Holly stiffened as she saw the girl who stood in the hall, her lovely face as pale as the white chrysanthemums on the polished top of the reception desk behind her.

She came slowly forward as Holly reached the bottom of the stairs. 'You're Holly, aren't you? I'm Vivienne,' she said. 'I do hope you—don't mind too much my calling like this.' She threw a little nervous glance backwards over her shoulder, as if she were expecting someone to come in through the front door. Jared? Holly wondered. He had wanted her to meet Vivienne; it would be like his high-handed arrogance to make sure that the meeting took place, whether she agreed or not. She could feel herself begin to bristle with annoyance; it really was too bad of him!

Vivienne said timidly, 'Don't be angry, please. Could we just talk together for a few minutes—in private?' She looked through the big double doors into the lounge, where the residents were grouped round the TV.

The dining room was empty, the tables already set for breakfast. 'Come in here,' said Holly, and led the way to the table by the window that she shared with one of the elderly widows who lived here permanently.

Vivienne sank into a chair. She was wearing a long dress in a misty mauve colour with a short mink jacket over it. Her great violet eyes had a sad, faraway look, her sleek black hair was brushed flat to her perfectly-shaped head. Holly felt numb inside. You wouldn't consider trying to compete with a girl who looked like this. Not if you were sane, you wouldn't. You'd be beaten before you began.

She sat down opposite and waited for the other girl to speak. After a moment Vivienne met Holly's eyes and looked away, putting a hand to her white throat. 'It's—difficult——' she began hesitantly. Then she seemed to make up her mind and rushed on, the words tumbling over each other. 'Jared has told me that you know all about me and—and Paul—and everything, so I won't say anything about that. It's all in the past now. I—I didn't think I could ever come back here after Paul and I split up in Mexico. I've been living with an aunt in the U.S.—in Boston. I thought I'd forget all about Jared and the way I'd treated him. I thought he'd probably have got another girl by now. But, you see, I couldn't forget.'

The great violet eyes were suddenly suffused with tears. 'I knew what an awful mistake I'd made, and I knew I still loved him. I *had* to come back—to see—to see if——'

'If he still loved you?' Holly put in drily.

'Yes, oh yes!' The girl clasped her hands together on the white tablecloth. 'I was so terribly afraid of meeting him again, I thought he'd be all bitter and cut me down to size, and I couldn't bear it if he did. But——' she smiled mistily '——he didn't, you know. He was so glad to see me again. And—and we've been able to take things up where we left off. But—but—and this is why I've had to see you—he seems to feel that he's in some way—sort of tied to you—that he has a duty to you——' Her eyes met Holly's pleadingly. 'It's—it's so difficult to explain——'

Holly regarded the lovely face with something like contempt. Heavens, the girl was wet! A beautiful, characterless—nothing. What were the words of that old song—'A doll I can carry, the girl that I marry must be.' Well, if that was what Jared wanted, good luck to him.

Soon she was going to weep for Jared, because, if she hadn't been crazy enough to refuse to marry him when he asked her, she might have been facing this girl now as Mrs Jared Kent. But she *had* refused and she had lost her chance.

Yes, soon she would weep, but for a little longer she had to play a part. 'What do you want me to say?' she asked, her lip curling slightly. 'That I haven't any claim on Jared? Well, I haven't. That he hasn't any duty towards me? He certainly hasn't. All that we are to each other is partners in a business sense—and that's only because it's been wished on both of us. I expect he's told you about that too, as you seem to know all about the situation.' Try as she might she couldn't keep the sharp bite out of her voice.

She stood up. 'And now I'm afraid I can't spare any more time. You may also know that I'm going abroad very soon on the firm's business, and I have rather a lot to do beforehand.'

The girl got to her feet hastily. 'Oh, of course, forgive me—I'll leave at once. I—I—I'm very grateful to you, Holly.'

Holly walked to the front door with her. Vivienne stood hesitating, biting her lip. 'Perhaps we could be friends some day?'

'Perhaps,' said Holly. 'Goodbye.'

The girl ran down the steps to a waiting car, which, in the light over the entrance, looked sleek and expensive. A woman with blue-rinsed hair sat at the wheel. This had evidently been a put-up job by Mummy—to find out how the land lay. Holly closed the door quickly; she didn't want to tangle with Vivienne's mother. She just wanted to get away from this place and everyone in it at the first possible moment. Since this last interview with Vivienne she was more determined than ever that somehow she must find a way to cut the knot that bound her to Jared. When she left here it must be for ever.

Jared insisted on driving her to Penrith to catch the London train, two days later. He was being so considerate, so thoughtful, it just wasn't true. Holly could only assume that he would be glad to see the last of her for a while. He would be thinking that by the time she returned he would be safely engaged to Vivienne and there would be no awkwardness for him in the situation.

He didn't know, of course, that she wasn't going to return.

Holly somehow managed to keep her shell of defence against him to the end. She was the cool,

sophisticated young woman executive, off on a sales
trip abroad. She looked the part too, her mirror had
assured her of that before she left. A small boutique
in Windermere had done her proud when she went
shopping yesterday. She wore a grey suit and a scarlet
silk blouse, with high black suede boots and a black
suede handbag. Her hair was brushed up smoothly
and wound into a chignon at the back of her head. The
whole effect was poised and elegant.

'You'll manage with your case?' Jared frowned as
they stood on the platform waiting for the train to
come in. 'I wish I could have driven you to the
airport. I don't like to think of you lugging this weight
around.'

'No problem,' Holly assured him casually. 'I'm
travelling light, as you can see.' The one case and a
small hand-satchel held everything that she needed to
take with her; the rest she would buy when she got to
Mexico. It was going to be a clean break. 'And Luis is
meeting me, of course. He'll look after me beautifully—
he's a pet.'

'I'm sure he is,' said Jared drily.

The train came rumbling in and he carried her case
to a first-class compartment and hoisted it on to the
luggage rack. He turned to her. 'Well, so long, Holly.
Have a good trip, and keep the flag of Kent and Son
flying in Mexico.'

'I will, I promise.' Panic struck her. He was going,
getting off the train, and she wouldn't see him again.
Perhaps never again. It was as if she were being carved
up into little pieces, the pain was almost physical. She
tried to photograph his face on her memory. She had
thought she wanted to forget him, but she knew at this
moment that he was there in her heart and no man
would ever take his place.

'I'll be in touch,' he said. She had already given him Juanita's address and phone number. 'I'll want to know how the sales campaign is getting on.' He gave her a quick hug and turned away and strode down the corridor, barging into passengers boarding the train. Holly saw him for a moment as he emerged on to the platform. He turned and lifted a hand towards her and then walked quickly away. He wasn't a man to linger over a goodbye.

It was lucky that Holly had the carriage to herself as far as Preston, because as soon as the train started the tears flooded out and wouldn't stop. By the time two elderly gentlemen got in she had managed to get herself at least partly under control, and if she felt the tears welling up again she put on dark glasses and went out into the corridor. It was a long, horrible journey, that seemed as if it would never end.

Once off the train it was better, because she had to keep her wits about her until she was finally installed on the plane. It wasn't until take-off that she looked down at the ground beneath and suddenly felt that she was leaving her heart behind, and started, uncontrollably, to weep again.

Luis was at the airport to meet her when her flight put down in Mexico City. He kissed her and held her at arm's length and studied her face. 'It is splendid to see you again, 'Olly, but you look very tired. I am so happy that you come. We will give you a wonderful time, Nita and I.'

Holly kissed him back. 'How are you, Luis? You look very smart.' It was good to see him again, with his humorous monkey-face and his immaculate pin-striped suit with a white shirt and a maroon silk tie.

She remembered that it was the done thing in Mexico City to dress very correctly. She had a quick picture of Jared in the casual cords and bush-jacket that he usually wore at the mill, and pushed it away. She mustn't keep thinking about Jared all the time—she mustn't.

Luis led her out of the airport building to where he had parked his car. 'Everything is going nicely. I 'ave three new accounts this week. I 'ave made several appointments for you later, when you are rested.' He helped her into the car with a gallant gesture; Holly thought that if he had worn a wide-brimmed hat he would have swept it off. What a nice little man he was—a little showy and ostentatious perhaps, but genuine and simple. What a difference from Jared Kent, who might possibly be genuine but was certainly not simple.

And what a difference Mexico was from the English Lake District! As they drove along the streets, with traffic snarling and tangling ferociously all around, Holly looked out of the car window at the passing scene and began to wonder how she would settle down again here among the noise and the petrol fumes and the smog that covered everything with a greyish haze. It was going to take a little time to adjust to the hectic pace of this huge city after the peace of Ambleside. She would take it slowly—she had all the time in the world, she told herself.

Luis drove straight to Juanita's flat in an exclusive custom-built block near Chapultepec Park. Juanita had just got in from her boutique, looking as elegant as ever in a fabulous suit of lilac and black. She embraced Holly warmly, enveloping her in a cloud of expensive perfume. 'We are so pleased to see you,

Holly. Sit down and rest—has it been a very long, boring journey?' Luis poured out drinks for them all and came and sat beside Holly on a deep cushioned sofa and brother and sister fired questions at her until Juanita said, 'But we are tiring you, *querida*. You must have a sleep after that long flight. Come along and I will show you your room—it is the same one that you had before. Then I will bring you a little tray with something nice to eat and you must sleep until you wake up. Say goodnight to Holly, Luis. You can talk plenty to her again tomorrow.' She linked her arm in Holly's and led her out of the room.

The roses were the first thing Holly saw when Juanita opened the door of her bedroom. 'Oh, how lovely!' She went across to where they stood in a black Aztec-decorated vase on the dressing table. Dark red roses, their perfume filling the small, luxurious room. 'But——' she began. Were they from Luis? She had heard the eagerness in his voice when he phoned her, seen the look in his eyes when he met her at the airport.

Then she saw the card, carefully written by the Interflora agent. 'Good luck to my highly-esteemed partner. Jared.'

'They were delivered this morning,' Juanita told her. 'You hafe a partner who sends you red roses, yes? That is *vairy* interesting.' Her black eyes twinkled knowingly.

Holly collapsed on to the bed, summoning up a yawn to cover the jolt she had had when she read the card. 'Oh no, Juanita, nothing like that. All in the way of business.'

But later, when she had eaten the delicious little tamales stuffed with chicken and drunk the glass of light wine that Juanita brought her on a tray, she slid out of bed and went over to the dressing table and buried her face in the red roses. Their velvet petals caressed her cheek, their scent was heavy in her nostrils and her sense of loss spread through her more sharply than ever before. It was understandable that Jared should want to boost her confidence on this marketing trip, and reasonable that he should choose this way to do it. He probably hadn't even specified the kind of flowers. She could almost hear him saying over the phone, as he ordered them, 'Oh, just send anything you've got.'

But why, thought Holly, her throat choked with misery, did it have to be red roses?

CHAPTER NINE

NEXT afternoon Juanita came home early from her boutique. 'I thought it would be nice to have a long gossip,' she said, busying herself with the coffee machine in the immaculate kitchen. Juanita spoke even better English than her brother; many of her customers were American.

Holly reached for the biscuit tin. 'I've been so lazy. I didn't hear you leave this morning, I must have slept until nearly midday.'

They sat in the window that looked out over the wide avenue leading to the park. 'That would do you good,' said Juanita. 'You looked so very tired last night, I worried for you. You are well, Holly?'

'Oh yes, I'm fine,' Holly said brightly. 'It's been a busy time lately, I've been learning the business. Did Luis tell you I'd taken over Paul's place as Marketing Manager of the company?'

Juanita nodded thoughtfully. 'Yes, that I knew. You enjoy it? You get on well with Paul's brother?'

Holly looked down into her coffee-mug. 'I didn't at first, he wasn't very—kind. You see, it turned out that I had inherited Paul's half of the Kent family business, and he hated that. He didn't want to be saddled with me for a partner. He didn't get on with Paul, you know.' No need to go into details with Juanita. She had been the first to help Holly when the accident happened; had gone with her to the hospital; had brought her back to this apartment, cold and shocked, after Paul was pronounced dead; had stood by her, with Luis's help, through all the legal matters, and the funeral arrangements. Yes, Juanita knew it all and she was loyal and compassionate.

Her dark eyes flashed now. 'That was no reason to be unkind to you. I should like to tell him——'

'Ssh!' Holly touched her hand. 'It's all over now. I've been learning to pull my weight in the business and we came to an—understanding.'

'An understanding?' the other girl put in eagerly. 'That is why he sends red roses?'

'No—no—I don't——' It was stupid the way her eyes flooded with tears. Would she never get over this weak, foolish yearning? She pulled out a handkerchief and blew her nose. 'Sorry,' she said. 'I think I've got a spot of jet-lag.'

Juanita was looking at her very thoughtfully. 'I guess it's something more than jet-lag. I guess you are in love, yes?'

Holly bit hard on her lip. 'Does it show so plainly?'

'Only to me, I know the signs. I have been in love myself,' Juanita added, her face a little sad. Juanita's husband had been a biologist and had died from a rare tropical disease over ten years ago. That was when Juanita had started her boutique. She had had boyfriends, but she had once told Holly that she would not marry again. 'It could never be the same,' she had said simply, and Holly knew how she felt.

'Do you want to tell me?' she asked Holly now, gently.

Holly shrugged. 'Not much to tell. The usual story—I fell in love and he—he's going to marry someone else. It's a bit more complicated than that, but that's the rough picture.'

'And "he" is this stepbrother of Paul's?'

'Yes, his name's Kent. Jared Kent.' Holly winced. Speaking his name made her ache inside.

Juanita's eyes were soft with sympathy. 'I am sorry, Holly, it is bad for you. But perhaps it will pass.' She didn't look very convinced. Was she thinking that love hadn't passed for her?

'Now look,' she said more brightly, after a moment or two. 'We must keep you very busy to take your mind off bad things. Luis has all sorts of plans—he is sure that you can make some killings, as he calls it, here in Mexico. And then you can go back and show this Jared what a wonderful partner he has got.'

Holly said nothing for almost a minute while she felt Juanita's eyes watching her anxiously. She looked down at her hands, lying limply on her lap as if there was no life in them.

'Juanita,' she said slowly at last, 'I don't see how I *can* go back. Not ever.'

For a week Holly filled every moment of the day and—thanks to Luis and Juanita—well into the night as well, for they insisted on taking her out to restaurants—to dance—to parties—or just to call on friends. In the daytime, with introductions from Luis, she visited firms and offices and interviewed potential customers, and while only two orders were clinched there were several firms who were definitely interested, and Holly would have had a heady feeling of satisfaction with the results of her efforts if only things had been different between herself and Jared. Even if they had been as they were before Vivienne came back.

Every evening he telephoned, and that didn't make

it any easier, because she ached inside for hours after
he had rung off. The calls were brief and all about
business, and he didn't sound particularly impressed
with the success she reported. Once or twice she tried
to prolong the call, just for the luxury of hearing his
voice a little longer. He had the kind of voice that the
telephone didn't alter at all—it came over the line deep
and velvety, just as if he were in the same room, and it
made her feel swimmy inside, as if she had drunk
strong wine.

'We all went to see the Ballet Folklorico yesterday,'
she told him on Friday. 'It was fabulous—the
wonderful colours of the costumes——'

'Really?' he cut her short. 'And who is "all"?'

'Well, just Juanita and Felipe, her boy-friend, and
Luis and I.'

'I'm glad you're enjoying yourself,' he said, but he
didn't sound interested. 'When are you thinking of
coming back?'

'Oh, not for several days, if that's O.K. with you.
I've got an appointment with a firm in Acapulco on
Tuesday I'm flying there on the shuttle service. It's
an up-market store and Luis has made contact with
them for me already. We may be on to a good thing
with them; apparently they have a local firm that
makes up exclusive fabrics for them and our PL200
line might be just right for bikinis and beach-wear,
Luis thinks.'

'Good,' he said briefly. And then, 'Is Ferida going
with you?'

'If he can get away. He's not sure yet.' Holly spoke
absently. She wanted to ask him about Vivienne, but
she didn't know how to put it, and he didn't mention
her. Surely he would tell her if he was engaged to be

married? Or was that to be taken for granted now that Vivienne had come back?

'You're flying back the same day? I'll ring you when you get back on Tuesday, then,' he said.

'Oh, don't bother, it might be quite late,' said Holly, 'and by the time I get in it will probably be the middle of the night for you.'

There was a click and the line went dead. She didn't know whether he had rung off or if they had been disconnected. She waited by the phone for a full five minutes, but he didn't ring back.

Luis telephoned from his apartment on the other side of the city on Monday evening. He was desolate, but he was negotiating an important deal and he couldn't possibly manage to get away next day.

'I am so very disappointed, 'Olly,' he mourned. 'I do not like to think of you alone there. I would so like to be with you in Acapulco, it is a so beautiful place. And romantic!' His little chuckle came over the phone. 'Your heart might 'ave softened towards me.'

That was only Luis's fooling, but it was a little too near the truth for comfort. 'I'm sorry too,' Holly said composedly, 'but don't worry. I know Acapulco quite well. I'll manage on my own.' Actually, she was rather pleased. It was becoming a little too obvious that Luis's interest in her wasn't purely one of business. Soon he would be making some sort of proposition, and she was going to find it awkward to turn him down. He was such a dear and he had been so kind to her. But as the plane came in to land and she saw below her the fabulous bays, the deep blue water, the rocks and palm trees and the great white hotels set against their green background of trees, she felt a curious twist inside and forgot all about Luis. Paul had brought her here for their honeymoon.

Honeymoon! it had turned into a nightmare. She wondered now if she could have known about Paul's drink problem before she married him. Perhaps a more worldly girl would have guessed. And perhaps a more worldly girl would have known that David Behrens was just using her. Perhaps a more worldly girl would be able to put Jared Kent out of her mind and out of her heart. She would work on it, she promised herself, she would work on it with every bit of resolution she could summon up.

She kept that resolution all through the day. The morning meeting went well and she knew that she was making a good impression on the prospective customers. When the buyer suggested that she should come back later in the day, after they had had time to discuss the matter between themselves, she felt she was almost home and dry. And sure enough, so it proved to be. By the end of the afternoon she had landed the most important order of her short career, and she was jubilant.

There was only one snag, and that was that it was too late now to get back today. She phoned Juanita at the boutique, to say she would be flying the following day.

'You will be O.K. there on your own?' Juanita sounded a little worried.

'No problem,' Holly said brightly. She was still buoyed up by her success with the order. 'I'm ringing from the Holiday Inn—I've been lucky to get a room here and I'll be lapped in luxury. Tell Luis I've had a terrific order from Señor Calvo if you see him. And Juanita——' She paused.

'*Si?*'

'Jared—Mr Kent—said he would phone. Would you explain what has happened if he does?'

'Of course. I will tell him your hotel and he can ring there if he wants.'

'No,' Holly said quickly. 'No, don't do that. I'm going to enjoy myself here and forget all about him,' she added firmly. If she said it often enough it might come true.

'Good for you,' laughed Juanita. 'Goodbye then, Holly. *Hasta la vista.*'

It would have been lovely to have gone out that evening and walked across the warm powdery sand to the sea, or watched the famous Quebrada divers who dive from the rocks a hundred feet up, with torches in their hands. Or just to have sat and drunk coffee and watched the myriad glittering lights reflected in the sea. But to go out—a girl alone! She knew better than that. So she was content to enjoy a solitary dinner in the restaurant, carefully avoiding the male glances of interest that came her way, and then retire to her room early.

Holly arrived back in Mexico City the next afternoon, having called again to finalise arrangements with her customers. She went straight to Juanita's boutique in the fashionable Zona Rosa and sat in Juanita's office, sipping tequila and recounting her adventures.

Juanita was delighted with her success but, as usual, wildly busy with her own business. When one of her sales-girls came in for the third time, looking worried, Holly said, 'Oh dear, I'm just getting in the way here. I'll get on the Metro and go back to your apartment. Then I'll stand you dinner to celebrate—and Luis too, if he's free. I can easily put in the time until you get home. I'll probably go along to the Museum of Anthropology—I didn't see one tenth of the wonderful things there last time I went.'

Back in the apartment she took a shower and changed into one of the new, light dresses she had bought at the boutique—a two-piece in a silky white material, with a bold pattern of poppy red. It was a sophisticated dress and one that she wouldn't have chosen before this trip, but somehow it had seemed to boost her confidence. As she strolled along the wide avenue through Chapultepec Park towards the Muscum she felt that she was winning her battle. She was riding high on a tide of success. She would stay and make this her home—for the time being anyway. Jared would have to make arrangements to replace her at the mill, if she wasn't there. Perhaps she would accept Juanita's offer of a job in the boutique, and as for Luis—well, she would take that as it came. She certainly wasn't ready yet to commit herself to a man again. She would be a career girl and like it.

Her smooth brown head held high under the warm Mexico sun, she climbed the wide steps to the Museum and into the huge open patio with its parasol-like cover, and from there began a tour of the lower halls. If she was going to make her home in Mexico she ought to learn something of its early history.

The halls were full of tourists, students, study-groups with their lecturers, but she was hardly aware of them. For an hour she concentrated on the exhibits: the chunky clay figures with their bulbous limbs and long, slitty eye-sockets. There was one of a woman kneeling, holding a little dog, which had sprung up into her arms. Holly stood for a long time looking at it. There was something so warm, so human about this tiny object that had been made more than two thousand years ago. She would find a photograph of it before she left.

There were exhibits from many different cultures, many different periods. There were vases with animal forms moulded into them—one shaped like a parrot, another like a turkey. From a later period there were jugs and pitchers and goblets, painted in earth colours of browns and fawns and creams and blues. There was gold jewellery—pins, necklaces, earrings. There was a huge monolith covered thickly with symbols—the famous Aztec calendar. She had seen that before, but it repaid a longer scrutiny.

And the gods! There seemed to be no end to them. All the civilisations had produced their own gods, it seemed. There were sun gods and jaguar gods, there was a god of renewal and a goddess of the young corn and there was the huge reclining rain god from Chichén Itzá.

She paused in front of a stone figure nearly three feet high, labelled 'Xochipilli', and read that he was the Aztec god of spring and love. He was rather wonderful; he had a diadem of feathers and his body was carved with flowers. He was sitting cross-legged, his hands resting on his knees, and he was looking up, as if in hope.

'Would you bring me the one I love?' Holly murmured, a wry grin touching her lips. 'What would I have to sacrifice?' Heavens, she thought, I'm going crazy.

She turned away, and suddenly she caught her breath. In the distance, among the crowd, she saw a man that looked like Jared. He had his back to her and he was walking away through an archway towards the next hall, but he was about the same height and his hair was dark and he moved deliberately, in the same way that Jared moved, as if he were in control of himself and everyone else around.

Her heart was beating uncomfortably, and she pulled a face at the stone god. 'That was quick work,' she said. 'But I don't think I'll stay for more.'

Hastily she retraced her steps to her first favourite—the statue of the kneeling woman with the dog. No threat here, this was warm and human. There was such a feeling of affection between the woman and the dog that was leaping up at her that Holly wanted to weep, and when a voice close behind her said quietly, 'Holly!' she spun round with a little cry, blinking away the tears.

Then it was as if her heart jumped right out of her body and she put out a hand blindly. 'Jared! What—what are you doing here? How did you find me?' The words came out like a croak.

'All in good time!' He had her firmly by the arm and was leading her towards the exit. 'Have you seen all you need to see here? I have, I promise you. I've been searching this damn place for hours, looking for you. If you've had all the culture you want let's get out.'

It couldn't be happening. It was just that wretched god up to his tricks—she must be hallucinating. She found herself out in the sunshine again and looked up, half afraid, but Jared was still there beside her.

'My hotel's only a short way from here,' he said brusquely. 'We'll walk.'

Holly drew in a deep unsteady breath. She knew this mood of Jared's and it was no good arguing with him or asking questions. She walked beside him and the sun was shining and the grass was freshly green and the usual Mexico City smog had disappeared. The world was new and sparkling just because he was there. He hadn't come to see her—it was business, of course, his tone told her that—but for the moment it was enough that he was beside her. She put out her hand and touched his arm as they walked, and he looked down enquiringly.

'I just wondered if you were real,' she smiled up at him uncertainly, and in the sunlight she saw the pallor under his brown skin, the lines of strain and weariness etched across his forehead and dragging at his mouth, the thick dark lashes almost brushing his cheeks, and her heart lurched inside her. 'I've been living in a world of ancient magic in there.'

'I'm real enough,' he said. 'I've come in a jet—no broomstick in sight.' He took her hand and tucked it through his arm and they walked in silence until he turned into the entrance of one of the plush hotels near the Park. He collected his key and they were wafted up in the lift to the fourth floor.

It was a luxurious room overlooking the Paseo de la Reforma, where the traffic glided past ceaselessly, far below. Holly stood at the window, her fingers digging into her palms, trying to think of something to say to break the silence, as Jared went across the room to pour out drinks. He seemed to be taking a long time about it and the silence was becoming almost painful.

'Have you come over to confirm all the lovely sales I've been making?' she chattered brightly. 'I haven't done at all badly, have I? I got on very well in Acapulco—you don't know about that yet, I'm really proud of myself and——'

She turned to him enquiringly. He was standing quite still looking at her, a glass in his hand. The room was almost silent, there was only the hum of the air-conditioner and the muted sound of traffic far below. Their eyes met and held in a long, long look, then he put down the glass and held out his arms and said,

'Holly,' in an odd, shaken voice, and she stumbled across the room and was held close to him, and his arms closed round her and he was kissing her and kissing her, murmuring, 'Sweetheart—darling—beloved——' over and over, and she was clinging to him and kissing him back, her arms locked round his neck.

There was no stopping now, for either of them. Jared drew her towards the big bed, his mouth still on hers, and lay beside her. After a moment or two his arms released her while he unzipped her dress and pulled it off. 'My love, I've waited so long for this,' he murmured thickly. 'All the way over on the plane—I couldn't stop thinking of it.'

Holly closed her eyes as he reached up and switched off the air-conditioner, then his hands came down again to her body and the last of her flimsy garments slipped from her. She felt him wrenching off his own clothes impatiently, and a moment later they were entwined flesh to flesh, clinging together, moving urgently against each other, moaning with the delight of it.

'I love you—love you——' he muttered over and over again, his mouth against her hair, his hands restless on her body, and then pressing her strongly to him as their passion rose together to its shattering fulfilment. And she echoed his words, crying out his name as the first pain was overcome by pleasure more intense than she had ever dreamed of.

Later, she lay for a long time quietly beside Jared as he slept, the lines of tiredness and strain wiped away from his face. She wasn't thinking at all, just feeling, and she felt warm and dreamy and as if all her skin was made of silk. And she was filled through and through by the sheer *wonder* of what had happened.

She didn't care why, or how, or what would happen
next. It was enough that Jared was lying here beside
her, one arm flung round her, heavy on her ribs, just
below her breast. She put out a hand and ran her
finger across his temple, at the margin of his dark hair,
and he sighed, stirred, and opened his eyes.

They smiled at each other. Then he levered himself
up on one elbow, looking down at her, frowning a little.
He said, 'My darling, was I too rough with you? I'd no
idea you were still a virgin. You're a widow, it never
occurred to me that you and Paul didn't make love.'

Holly turned her head on the pillow, away from
him. After a moment she said very quietly, 'I think he
was—pretty far gone when I married him. I never
guessed. I must have been very naïve. He told me he
loved me, but I think now that he must have been
frightened; he must have known what was happening
to him, although he would never admit it. Afterwards,
when I realised the truth, I tried my best to get him to
stop drinking—to get help—to go to a doctor or a
clinic, but he wouldn't.' Her eyes closed on the
memory of those awful scenes.

Jared's face was grim. 'I suppose he wanted
someone kind and sympathetic to lean on and look
after him. He met you and saw all the qualities in you
that he needed.'

'I did what I could,' said Holly.

He smoothed her hair back from her face very
gently. 'Poor sweet, you had a bad time. And he didn't
even make love to you.'

'He—couldn't,' Holly said simply.

He groaned as he took her in his arms. 'It's over
now, my dearest one,' he murmured. 'I'll try to make
it up to you—for everything. For my own abominable

behaviour—even for my stepbrother's shortcomings, the poor devil.'

'He wasn't really bad,' Holly mused. 'Only weak. He didn't have a father, and Blanche wouldn't be the best kind of mother to bring up a son.'

Jared laughed grimly. 'You can say that again! I could say, "There but for the grace of God go I".'

'You!' Holly scoffed. 'Nothing in your upbringing could have made you anything but a——'

'——a bullying, dictatorial chauvinistic tyrant?' he said wryly.

'Did I say that?'

'I'm not sure those were the exact words, but I bet that was what you were thinking. You hated my guts. Later on I consoled myself with the thought that it might be a good sign, that if you hadn't cared at all you wouldn't have bothered to notice me.'

'Notice you?' she squealed. 'How could I fail to notice you? From that very first moment when I saw you standing at Heathrow looking all arrogant and dismissive, you got straight into my bloodstream and stayed there, like a virus.'

'Charming!' He laughed and his hand began to wander over her shoulders and mould itself to the swelling curves of her breast.

Holly shivered, but she went on doggedly, 'And you saw me and thought, My God, have I got to put up with this terrible female? Right?'

'Wrong,' he said, and his hand was moving downwards now to stroke her flat stomach.

Her back arched itself at his touch, but with a tremendous effort she forced herself to lie still. 'You were so beastly to me. You went out of your way to hurt me.'

He groaned. 'Not you, my love, but the girl who was Paul's wife, who'd come to disrupt my life. And by God, you did,' he added, drawing her close against him. 'The same virus must have attacked me when I saw you standing there in that silly little black hat, looking so lost and so determined to be dignified. I fell in love with you then, though it took me a little time to admit it to myself, and it's been growing ever since. I want you with me for good, I'm only half alive when you're not with me.'

His hands were moving over her more urgently now. He said, his voice husky, 'It seems to be one of those viruses that keep recurring frequently. Oh, darling, trust me, I promise it will be better this time.'

'Could it be?' she said, smiling up into his eyes that held such a blaze of tenderness that she caught her breath as she reached up and drew him down to her.

It was dark by the time they were ready to face the world again. Holly, glowing from her shower and sparkling with joy, sat in front of the dressing table in her white and poppy-red dress, putting the finishing touches to her hair, and called through to the shower-room, 'I'd better ring Juanita—she'll be wondering where I've got to.'

Jared emerged, a green towel knotted round his waist, his hair damp, his chin smooth, exuding an odour of after-shave lotion. She saw him through the mirror and her inside lurched. 'I doubt it,' he said. 'She struck me as a very intelligent lady.'

'You've seen her?'

'Oh yes, indeed. I telephoned Luis Ferida's office when I arrived. He didn't sound awfully chuffed, but eventually he directed me to his sister's boutique. I went along to the Zona Rosa and Juanita and I had a—

very interesting talk.' He concentrated upon pulling up his second sock.

Holly carefully tucked back a strand of mink-brown hair. 'What's that supposed to mean?'

'She—er—implied that her brother Luis was about to throw his hat into the ring, so to speak, and that if I had any intention of staking a claim to you I'd better look slippy about it. She speaks very good English, does your friend Juanita. She said I might find you at the Museum, so I hustled along there and started my search. God, what a place! How many square miles does it cover? I'd been travelling for about thirty-six hours already and I was just about to sit down and weep when I saw you.'

She turned slowly on the dressing-stool. 'But I don't understand—why did you have to rush out here to Mexico? Weren't you happy with the work I was doing? Did you come to check up on me?'

He laughed. 'You bet I came to check up on you! Those phone calls had me shaking in my shoes. Evenings out with this macho Ferida fellow—dinners, dancing—I didn't like the sound of it all—and when you said you were off to Acapulco with him I knew the time had come to act. I left Bert Gregg in charge and got on the first flight I could.'

Holly turned back to the mirror. 'Luis couldn't come to Acapulco. I went on my own.'

He pulled on his trousers and came across to her. 'Well, that's a relief.' He put both hands on her shoulders and spun her round to face him. 'You're not really hooked on the bloke, are you? Even mildly?'

She dimpled. 'Luis is a sweetie, I like him very much.'

'*Like?* That's all? Promise me that's all?' His hands

moved and tightened on her throat. 'It's me you love—tell me that.'

'It's you I love,' she said obediently.

He lifted her to her feet and drew her close against his damp body. 'Now tell me properly,' he demanded.

'Oh, Jared——' there were tears in her eyes '—you're a bully and a tyrant and I love you. I adore you and I always will.'

'And you'll marry me—just as soon as we can manage to arrange it?'

'Of course,' she murmured. Then, suddenly, it was all too much. Joy overwhelmed her. She flung her arms round his neck. 'Oh, I'm so happy, so happy,' she wept. 'I thought you were going to marry Vivienne. You s-said you loved her.'

'I did—once,' he said soberly as they sat side by side on the bed. 'I'd thought so long about her coming back—and then—when she turned up that night, it threw me completely. I was all set to ask you again to marry me and I thought that this time you might say yes. Then—wham!—up pops Vivienne and I was thrown off course. She—and her mother—made it plain what they wanted. I took her out once or twice and all the time I kept thinking of you. And you seemed so distant again. I thought you might have got over our previous—er—difficulties, but there you were—the cool young woman executive, light years away from me, behind a high wall. When this Mexican trip came up I thought it might be as well if you went—it might clear the air.'

'And did it?' whispered Holly.

'You bet it did! Within a couple of days Vivienne and her mother had left for the South of France, having given me up as a bad job. Vivienne's a lovely girl and has about as much spark in her as a wet squib—I wondered I'd never seen that before. Her mother's one aim in life is to be some man's mother-in-law. But not mine—heaven forbid!' He shuddered.

Holly was quiet for a time. Then she said slowly, 'I'd like to go back home.'

Jared laughed triumphantly and drew her close until her head rested on his shoulder. 'Home—that's a lovely word. It was snowing when I left—you'll find a big difference from the climate here.'

She nodded. 'I know. Mexico's a grand place—fascinating—but I love it there. I love the old house and the mountains and the lakes and views from the window—and Paws—and I might even grow to love Mrs Burkett.' She giggled. 'And it'll be super there in the spring, won't it?' Her voice was dreamy. 'I'll make lots of friends and we can have parties now and again. And—Jared—I can go on working with you, can't I? We'll still be partners?'

'We'll always be partners,' he said. 'That particular knot can't be untied, praise be. And you can go on working as long as you want, of course—on one condition. No, two conditions.'

'Which are——?'

'First, that when you go abroad we go together.'

Her eyes danced. 'Lovely—no problem. And the other?'

'Well——' he drawled slowly, 'it just occurred to me that there's a vacant place in the family firm that even you can't fill.'

She turned questioning eyes on him and he smiled into them. She wondered how she could ever have thought those eyes cold and bleak. They were filled with tenderness now.

'When you grow tired of being a successful business woman, my love, we might fill the vacancy together.'

'I don't quite understand,' Holly wrinkled her forehead.

He laughed softly, 'The family firm has always been Kent—and Son. See what I mean? That's where the vacancy is at present.'

She felt her cheeks go warm. 'I see,' she whispered. 'I'll do my best to remedy that, if you will.'

His deep laughter filled the quiet room. 'Try and stop me,' he said.

Coming next month in Harlequin Romances!

2683 ISLAND OF DOLPHINS Lillian Cheatham
Instead of being welcomed to the tiny Caribbean island of Tamassee,
a research assistant is treated like an intruder in a millionaire's
private paradise.

2684 NO LAST SONG Ann Charlton
First impressions are often deceiving. But what can a young
musician do to convince an Australian tycoon she is not a ne'er-do-
well out to hoodwink his favorite aunt?

2685 LOVE'S GOOD FORTUNE Louise Harris
An art student, heiress to millions, is pleased when a critically-
acclaimed painter seems genuinely interested in her and not just her
fortune—until he jumps at her rather hasty proposal.

2686 LAKE HAUPIRI MOON Mary Moore
Any man who would even contemplate marriage without love is
surefire trouble. So a young nurse pretends she's otherwise engaged
when she falls in love with a disillusioned New Zealand
sheep-station owner. .

2687 NO HONOURABLE COMPROMISE Jessica Steele
All's fair in love and war. And when a business tycoon snatches a
place on the board of directors from the company owner's daughter,
she plans a major offensive to dishonor him—only to have it blow up
in her face.

2688 WINTER IN JULY Essie Summers
Determined to discover the reason for her father's exile from New
Zealand, a Scottish nurse goes undercover and unearths an injustice
that threatens her future with the man she loves.

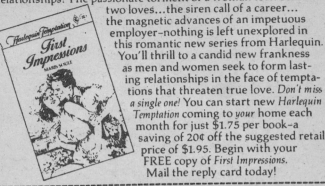